SWEET ANGEL BAND

Winner of the 1991 Willa Cather Fiction Prize

The Willa Cather Fiction Prize was established this year
by Helicon Nine, Inc., and will be awarded annually to a previously
unpublished manuscript chosen by a distinguished writer
through an open, nationwide competition

The judge for 1991 was Robley Wilson.

SWEET ANGEL BAND

&

Other Stories

R. M. KINDER

HELICON NINE EDITIONS
KANSAS CITY, MISSOURI

All rights reserved under International and Pan-American Copyright
Conventions. Published by Helicon Nine, Inc., Kansas City, Missouri.
Grateful acknowledgment is made to the editors
of the following publications, in which some of the stories herein
originally appeared, sometimes in slightly different form:
Cimarron Review: "Sweet Angel Band";
Cottonwood Review: "Bloodlines";
CutBank: "With a Change of Seasons."
Dickinson Review: "The Prowler";
The Nebraska Review: "The Vernacular";
New Times: "Baptism";
Primavera: "Cora's Room";
Puerto del Sol: "Bootheel";
South Dakota Review: "Craryville Box"

Cover: Thomas Hart Benton: *Lord, Heal the Child*, 1934.
Egg tempera and oil on canvas. Loan from John Callison
to the Nelson-Atkins Museum of Art, Kansas City.
Book design by Tim Barnhart

Partial funding for this project has been provided by
the Missouri Arts Council and
the Kansas Arts Commission, state agencies;
and by the N.W. Dible Co.

Library of Congress Catalog Number: 91-65863

ISBN: 0-962740-2-9

Printed in the United States of America
by Boelte-Hall Litho, Roeland Park, Kansas

FIRST EDITION

Helicon Nine Editions • P.O.Box 22412 • Kansas City, MO 64113

To Glenneth Jewell Goff Robison
and all her family

CONTENTS

Baptism

Both windows of the kitchen were open, unscreened, and clusters of insects periodically appeared like tiny whirlwinds, coming from the darkness toward the light. The girl at the table watched them when her mother wasn't talking, as now, and only the sound of the radio, the *Gospel Quartet Hour*, filled the quiet. She was a small child, nine, and thin past just being fragile. The arms wrapped around her shins, holding knees as a chin rest, were like the fine lines of an oriental sketch with no flesh. Her hair was dark red, the same color as her mother's only the girl's was braided into wide ropes that curved from the thickness and spring of the contained hair into the shape of sheephorns. Her eyes were dark blue, almost black, and the white that surrounded the irises was clear, forming such a contrast that she always appeared startled.

Her name was Lee Ann and she was worried, at the moment, about three things: the canker sore on the inside of her left cheek which she touched from time to time with her tongue, sure it was spreading, had spread just since supper time; the approaching bedtime hour; and whether or not her mother would let her get baptized on Sunday morning. If she could get baptized on Sunday, then she might not have to go to the doctor about the canker sore.

"Lee Ann, honey, turn that fan off or around, will you? It's drying out the clothes."

Lee Ann switched off the fan, counted how long it took for the blades to wind down. She pushed her tongue into her cheek again, watched her mother slip the yoke of the man's white shirt over the tip of the ironing board. On the radio the jubilant voices of men who all sounded fat to Lee Ann were singing "Joshua Fit the Battle Round Jericho." She thought they would all look like Brother Fulkerson who led most of the songs at the church she and her mother attended; he was, she believed, at least five hundred pounds and sang as deep as an elephant, and he wouldn't kneel to pray. He said you should stand in front of a King. That had bothered Lee Ann for a while, especially at night when she said her prayers from the safety of her bed. She believed the Devil got under her bed at night, so she couldn't kneel. She hoped God understood that. She didn't think he understood very much.

"I don't think I can keep this up." Her mother moved away from the ironing board toward the stove and coffee pot that was there from the time Lee Ann got up in the morning till bedtime. "My arms get so tired. Sometimes at work they feel so weak I can't stack the boxes."

"Get old Myrtle to stack for you. She does it for Beth Wilson."

"You know how they are. Wash each other's back. Nobody does that for me. Never did and never will. Did I tell you Beth's girl is pregnant?"

Lee Ann nodded. Her mother lifted the dish covering the skillet on the stove, broke off a piece of the leftover liver and stood chewing.

"I only fixed the liver 'cause I thought he'd be come home for supper. I know you don't like it, honey."

"It's okay."

"He said he'd be here."

"The gravy was good."

"You want some oatmeal before you go to bed?"

Lee Ann held her knees tighter, shook her head no. "It's only eight-thirty."

"Seems later." Her mother came toward the table, cup in hand, sighing. "Lord. If I can just rest for a while, maybe I can get it done tonight, the ironing. Have tomorrow to clean the house. Maybe your dad will stay home. We can go to a movie maybe."

The edges of the canker sore were ridges now and the tip of her tongue was hurting too. She rubbed her finger against it; there were tiny dots all over the tip.

"Why do you think he does this? I mean, it's not like we ask very much. Even the night you were born. My brother had to haul him out of that place."

If the canker sore spread to her tongue she would be unable to eat. Maybe she would lose her tongue.

"Do canker sores eat all the way through?"

"You been using that hydrogen peroxide?"

"It burns."

"You been using it?"

"I think I need to go see Doctor Parks."

"There's nothing wrong with you, Lee Ann, for me to spend two dollars. You know how hard I work to earn two dollars? You use that peroxide like I told you and you'll be fine." The last words were lower and her mother's eyes were drooping. Lee Ann knew what was coming.

"Don't go to sleep," she said.

"Lord, honey, I have to, just for a minute. Seems like I been working all my life." She pushed the cup aside, lowered her head onto her folded arms. "All my life," she said.

On the radio a man was talking now, but there was singing behind his voice and words sort of rose and fell in time. With her mother sleeping, the house was too quiet, like at night. When everyone was asleep, it was like you were the only one alive, the only one anything could watch move. Lee Ann looked from the dark red curls of her mother's hair down the hallway toward the living room. It was a black cave; her bedroom was on the other side. To her left, the air through the window seemed cooler; Lee Ann glanced at it from the corner of her eyes, then at the clock shaped like a chicken hanging above the stove. Almost nine o'clock. If he weren't home in a few minutes she would have to start or she couldn't get everything done by ten.

The voices on the radio were praying now. Lee Ann bowed her head, pressing her cheekbones against her knees, but leaving slits in her eyes. When they began singing again, she kept her head bowed, to make up for the open eyes. If He was any good, like everyone said He was, He shouldn't make her mother work so hard that she fell asleep like this. Sometimes she fell asleep in the living room, too. But then she had been working since she was twelve. "Dad made me quit school when Momma died, honey. Mrs. Graham, my teacher, she went to him and offered to have me for the next year, I could help her she said, but he said no." Lee Ann looked briefly at the sleeping woman across from her. The mouth was slack, moist. The eyes didn't seem to be closed all the way. At night, when Lee Ann got frightened enough to risk waking her mother, she tried never to look at the face until she had shaken her. It seemed different, sleeping, the eyes all sunken back behind the cheekbones; looked like a devil face. Lee Ann shivered, lowered her legs to the floor slowly. It was nine o'clock.

At the door from the porch to the back yard and the outhouse beyond, Lee Ann stopped. Behind her the angle of light from the kitchen came only part way across the wooden floor. She couldn't use a flashlight; it was against her rules. On the steps outside she began, moving her lips with her thoughts, but not speaking: nails, claws, hammer, wood, keep me safe, keep me good. She thought it three times to the wood structure. If her mother were awake she could look back at the kitchen and maybe see her moving, her singing, but if she turned now, Lee Ann didn't know what might be in the house, maybe her mother's sleeping face, only awake, at the window. She pulled the latch, stepped inside and walked the narrow feet to the back. She sat down, holding her panties with both hands just below the knees. She couldn't go. She waited. Bits of moonlight lay in splinters over the floor. The branches of the tree behind the outhouse scraped over the roof, but she didn't jump. The first time she had, but then she couldn't remember when the first time was. When the few warm drops of urine finally came, she cleaned herself and, in the yard again, began: nails, claws, hammer, wood, keep me safe, keep me good. She only had to do it twice more and she could go to bed.

Her mother was still at the table, one arm dangling down at

her side, mouth completely open. Lee Ann turned the fire on under the coffee pot again. She sucked on her cheek as she lifted the ironing board, released the legs and folded them back, stuck the board between the refrigerator and wall. If her mouth wasn't better by tomorrow, she'd ask her dad for two dollars; if he came home. Sometimes he didn't. She took the stack of folded shirts down the hallway, turning on the light in each room before she entered. It was just the soul they worried about, God and the Devil, and she wished she didn't have one. She wished she could give it up. One night she wanted to say so, but she was afraid they would come get it. But Sunday she was going to. Her mother told her children didn't need to be baptized, because they didn't go to hell; her mother said He loved children. Her mother had had to sleep alone many nights when she was a child, and since. "You tore me so bad, honey. It took a long time for me to heal; but I loved you so. You made up for everything. You mattered so much to me I didn't care if he took off." She was going to ask for the two dollars tonight. Her mouth burned.

By the time she rinsed out her mother's cup, wiping away the dark stain line where the cold coffee had lowered, and poured more, it was nine-twenty. On the radio they were singing about Jordan, not crossing Jordan alone. Lee Ann knew that song. She set the cup down quietly, a few inches away from her mother's hand. "Momma," she whispered. "Momma," standing behind the chair, but there was no response. The light from the windows seemed to stop right outside, against a wall of black. Preacher Wilson said when you were baptized, you gave your soul to God and all your sins were washed away, but the Devil would keep coming around trying to get it back. She didn't understand why he would come around her if God had the soul. "Momma," she said one more time, then sighed, and turned to the porch.

This time the moon slivers were farther back, like they had been pushed. They were right at her feet and it took her a long time to go, watching them to see if they moved. Outside again, she heard voices, and looked toward the house. He had come home. She could see him standing in the hallway door to the kitchen, one arm out, saying something down toward the table. Now she didn't have to do it. That was part of the rule. If he was in the house, she didn't have to do it. But she bowed her head anyhow; she was already there, it would be an extra one for later on, for tomorrow night, before Sunday.

The food in the skillet was being warmed. Her mother stood next to the stove, arms folded beneath her breasts.

"You go on to bed, honey," she whispered.

He was just sitting down, putting elbows to the table first, before lowering his body into the chair. He pulled cigarettes from his pocket, fumbled one out.

"Goddamn. Come home hungry. Work all week. Goddamn."

"Lee Ann." She felt her mother's hand pushing her. "Go on. You were a sweet thing, putting away the ironing."

His head was weaving as she passed, watching her. He reached out, pulled her to him. "Say hello to your daddy. Your momma's mad at him. What you been doing all day? Huh? You been taking care of yourself all day?"

Lee Ann nodded.

"You been a good kid?"

She nodded again.

"That's my girl. That's my girl." He glared across the room, hugged Lee Ann.

"I got a canker sore," Lee Ann said.

"You what?"

She turned in his arm so her mother couldn't see her.

"I got a canker sore. Here." She pulled out her cheek with her finger. "I want to see Doctor Parks, but Momma won't give me two dollars."

"Well, I will. I'll give my baby whatever she wants."

He let go of her to dig in his pocket, taking out crumpled bills which he dropped on the table with the change, letting it ring while he glared across the room again.

"You take anything you need, sugar."

14

Lee Ann took two dollars and ran down the hall.

In her bedroom she removed her clothes and folded them on the chair. The shorts had to be folded three times, and the shirt, any buttons toward the back, even if he was home. The shoes had to be pointed to the doorway, socks rolled inside. She slipped into her nightgown and left the back unbuttoned while she unbraided her hair. The money she put beneath her pillow. His voice down the hallway was alternately loud then fading, as if he could not hold up his head to say the whole thing. Lee Ann didn't need to be in there to see. But he wouldn't be that way in the morning; she knew that. And then there was just tomorrow night and then Sunday. She opened the window by the bed, pushed the small block beneath it and lay down. The crickets outside were singing. They never sang when she went outside before bed. She understood why. It had to do with God and her. She turned onto her side. Her mother had never been able to go to church when she was a little girl. Her mother had had to quit school at twelve and stay with old people who were dying and they paid her father. She touched the money, clutching it in her hands. She pulled her knees up to her chest. Tonight she didn't have to pray, but she wanted to.

"Lee Ann."

She felt her mother's weight on the bed, the hand on her shoulder.

"Lee Ann?"

The words seemed to curl up in Lee Ann's stomach. She turned over slowly, pulling the two dollars out.

"I don't want it, honey. It's okay. I just wanted to make sure you were all right. Unbraided your hair and all. You can go see Doctor Parks. He's probably open tomorrow." She drew Lee Ann up, held her. "It's just because I was so tired, honey. I get cranky when I'm tired."

Lee Ann pushed her fist against the softness of her mother's breast. "I want to be baptized, Momma. I want to be baptized on Sunday."

Bloodlines

There was a time when I thought Jack Defoe had it better than any one else in the world; and then there was a time when I knew for sure he'd be one of those people who can't ever find their place. I could see him shooting someone some day when he grew up, or even before. Maybe he worried about it, too. We were only ten then, and a lot of the things we worried about we didn't talk about, or could only mention in a few words, just having to accept that the other one understood that nothing at all would have been said if it hadn't mattered pretty much.

We lived in one of those small towns they make movies about now, as if such towns existed only in the past and weren't still all over the country. Everyone knew everyone, and most of their past. Relationships mattered as much as names, because the thickness of the blood passing down accounted for a lot. "You know Michael's aunt on his mother's side? When she was fifteen, she stood up in church and cursed the preacher." That would be an explanation for why I skipped out of church every time I could. It didn't directly accuse my mother, or me, of being sinful, but it kept the reason in the family where it belonged.

Jack Defoe had a pretty good family on his father's side as far as making money; being successful in an area that could boast only a factory and the standard small town street stores: one dime store, which was also the pharmacy, one cleaner's (at that time—it closed within a year; people washed and hung things on a line outside), a Western Auto, Defoe's Store, Sandy's Tavern and Wilson's Cafe. His family had owned Defoe's Store probably as long as the town had existed, and William Defoe, Jack's father, had enough sense to stock it from St. Louis and run ads in the local paper (Dexter's), that said so. He sat as an Elder in the Baptist church, and when he decided to run for mayor he took to sitting in Sandy's tavern until after the election. He wasn't a drinker, though, or a bad man, although my mother never liked him. He took Jack with him on trips and he invited me over a lot, and other kids, and would play softball with us or tell us stories. Their house was not really fancy, at least not the way the money would probably allow, but it was better than I or most of the kids knew. It was the old Snyder house. It had French doors going between the bedrooms, and a porch that curved all the way around. And behind it, though they were crumbling, were stalls where horses used to be kept. Once Jack wrote me a deed for two of those stalls—we had seen a western in Dexter about deeds to land— because I didn't like to play with anything that wasn't mine. I was a little bit sensitive around Jack about not having anything and about being one of the Hayes. Even if I couldn't have expressed it, I knew being one of the Hayes meant coming from a drinking line, and women that had more babies than they would ever have room for in the house or money for in their lives.

So I, and the others, too, I think, envied Jack his father. And maybe found it bearable because he had the mother he did. She was one of those people who are described later, after they've died and a gracious judgment is a sign of the speaker's worth, as being a gentle person. She hummed most of the time, went barefoot in a housedress—always clean, but usually beltless. No matter the money or the clothes or the occasion, she always looked plain, when really she wasn't. She had those fine bone features that some people have only as they grow older and the skin seems to have tightened from the years, and soft, brown hair. She was always giving things away, even new items. Every time the church had an auction, she came up with a box of things that the church ladies took without ever putting up for bid. And if any of us kids ever admired anything Jack had, and she was within hearing, she'd say, "Why don't you give that to him, Jack? He'd probably like it better than you do."

But she just didn't fit with William. And the Defoes, besides, had a history of chasing women. So I guess we kids knew about

17

the trouble before Jack, since our parents could, and did, talk about it around the supper table, or afterwards. We knew he had been asked to step down as Elder. The Sunday the preacher made the announcement about William resigning, Bobby Wilson turned around to look at me and wrinkled his nose. We knew. It had something to do with a woman who taught school over in Puxico, and she had resigned, too.

So when Jack told us one day, hunched back in the corner of one of the stables, that his dad was gone, we didn't say anything at all. We watched him trying to roll a cigarette on one of those mechanical rollers they used to have. He was awkward with it that day, but later on, he would roll a whole box full of cigarettes, and sell them at school for a nickel apiece. He had William Defoe's blood all right. When the carnival came to town (once a year in September—the churches always held their revivals then, which is when I'd skip out of church the most) Jack would stand at a booth until he figured out which prizes people liked the best. Then, when the carnival was ready to leave, he'd buy a bunch of little things, like those Japanese letter openers, and then sell them to the kids at school. Jack always had money.

It was after his dad (and the teacher, too, according to supper table talk) had gone to St. Louis, and a store manager came in for Defoe's Store, that Jack started treating his mother in a way most of us didn't like. She used to, for example, take store-bought cookies, put a little marshmallow cream on them and stick them in the oven for a minute and serve them with koolaid. "I don't see why you can't just buy marshmallow cookies," Jack'd say. Or maybe he'd say, "Where's your belt?" and she would look at him for a minute. I got the feeling that maybe he had picked up some of those things from William, and I sort of liked my own father a little more. He was in his cups from time to time, but he never let one of us even look cross-eyed at my mother.

Then Jack started with the war souvenirs. His dad sent him a couple of boxes filled with odds and ends from his army days:

some postcards bought in Paris, some foreign money. Jack put them all on pieces of velvet he bought at the dime store and hung them on the wall. Bobby Wilson and I worried about the nails he put in the wall that Saturday while his mother was gone, but he said she didn't give a damn. And I guess she didn't, or I guessed then she didn't. Because he expanded that collection far past the content of the boxes. He rode with me and my dad to the Cape one day, when I had to have a tooth out—Witch Hazel wouldn't work and I wasn't sleeping—and while I was in the dentist's office, Jack made the rounds of war surplus stores. He had a bayonet, canteen, some kind of sword, and more medals, and he hung every one of them on his wall.

He took to smoking his own cigarettes when we sat back in the stables devising what he called war games. That was when he looked like William. He caught beetles or grasshoppers and interrogated them. He'd lean back, pull one leg off a beetle and see if it could still walk; tie some thread behind that round button of a grasshopper's head and either hang it from a nail or just pull the thread tighter until the head came off. Once we were sitting at the opening of the stall when Jack's mother came out to put up some clothes. Jack had piled a little mound of dirt and had it almost covered with black beetles, each pinned to what Jack called an attack position by one of the straight pins he had found in his mother's sewing machine. His mother didn't gag, but she stared right at him in such a way that I said I had to go home and I didn't go back for a few days.

She didn't whip him though. I asked about that, and there was no cause for him to be lying when he said no. He even said it like it disgusted him, as if she couldn't do that. And she couldn't. He'd say things like "What do you do with the money Dad sends?" And she wouldn't even answer him. She went to work at the factory, somewhere near my mother's line. And Bobby Wilson said his parents told him she put those checks from William right into the bank; never touched the money, either.

One Sunday Jack asked me to help him find some leeches.

It's not hard to do when it's been raining, and really not hard when it hasn't. In our classroom in the church basement, sometimes they were crawling around the edges of the room where the concrete seemed to hold water year round and keep little pools in the corner. So Jack and I just went through the drainage ditches behind the main house streets and got a jarful of the black things. I've never liked them because they won't hold their shape. Something that always looks the same you can get used to or at least know what it is. Like it's a round creature. But a leech changes. It can be roundish and flat, or flat and thin, and one minute it can be short and the next long and skinny in the water. But we got a lot of them, and we took them back to his place.

Even not liking leeches, though, I didn't care much for what Jack did. He pulled rocks up, and not by the stables either. He pushed a mound of rocks up near the house, out from the shade of the oak tree near their kitchen window. He went in the house, and I noticed that he let that screen door slam pretty hard. I was nervous about his mother even if he wasn't. When he came out, he had a magnifying glass in his hand. He took a thickish twig from the tree, scraped out one of those leeches and held it with the twig against the rock. Then he caught the sun in that magnifying glass and kept it there. It made me hurt a little, the way that leech squirmed. I guess it would have squirmed anyhow, it's in their nature, the way they move anytime, but it kept looking drier and drier and changed color and I knew it was being cooked slow. I told him I had to go and he called me a yellowbelly. It was what we said then. So I stayed for one or two more, but what I watched was the kitchen window. I saw her just once, but I didn't hear the door even though I waited a while on the other side of the house.

That night I mentioned it at supper, just asking my folks if they knew what Jack Defoe did today, in that way that means maybe I heard about it. My mother gave a little shiver and said he sure was a Defoe, and then she went on in that running spiel she has when she doesn't like something, about how of course every living creature in the world felt pain, and how she still got sick over those fish she had scalded. My grandma, who is referred to by my mother as a tough old lady, told Momma that scalding fish killed them quick and made them scale easy. Momma tried it and when the fish kept trying to jump out of the water until they finally died, she ran out into the back yard and cried and stomped her foot over and over. She's only been to the eighth grade, like my father, and she didn't always act like everyone else's mother, but she was o.k. She's close to eighty now and she still says, Michael, you should go to church; you should take your boy to church. Then she'll add that I didn't turn out so bad.

I didn't even ask Jack about the leeches, but I knew she hadn't done anything, because when he and Bobby finally came to get me and we walked through his back yard toward the house, the pile of rocks was still there, with brown stains all over it. That day we just talked, although Jack smoked, and Bobby and I did, too. Jack told us how he thought he might be going to live in St. Louis, and he didn't like it here anymore and his mother made him sick. He said she "muled" around. I told him my mother muled around, too, and it made me sick sometimes. Bobby said his did, too. Then Jack told us his mother's birthday was on Sunday and he was going to make her present.

I think Bobby and I both knew what kind of present it would be, but we both went to the party anyhow. I took a handkerchief, which is what my mother said I should take, and she ambled on about what a poor choice that girl had made and if I'd let her know in time she would have picked up a Testament, just as a sign sort of. Bobby was there and me, and Jack's grandma and aunt, both of them with hair down to their waist, although where we were raised women over thirty are supposed to keep hair short or up. We had koolaid and homemade cake and ice cream, while the women had coffee and cake, and then she opened the gifts. She opened mine first and it embarrassed me being so little until I saw that what her mother had given her was a homemade dress and her sister had given her a box of three oranges covered with cloves and red ribbon stuck to them for hanging and making the house smell sweet. We had one hung right by the kitchen stove.

Jack's present was a necklace. At first it looked like one of those seashell necklaces from the dime store, made in California, and I felt good for him that he had chosen that. But the expression on Bobby's face made me look again, and then I saw what Jack had done. They were shells, all right, but snail shells, like the kind that were in everyone's back yard at times. And I knew he hadn't searched for empty, whole ones. She knew, too. She put the necklace on the table and stared at it for a while, then took a deep breath. She had never looked at Jack. Then she turned to her mother and asked if they still raised chickens, and if so, would they mind going and getting one, right now, if it wasn't too much trouble, and bringing it back? She'd pay them for it. They didn't seem to understand, but they didn't question her either. Jack just sat at the table watching his mother. She cut more cake and put it in front of us with a spoonful of ice cream beside each piece and began clearing up.

"We're going to the stables," Jack said.

"No. You're not."

Bobby Wilson and I started eating our ice cream, or mashing it around, and not one of us left the table for the hour or so it took them to come back. The table was clean except for the necklace which lay right where she left it. When we heard the truck pull into the driveway, she disappeared for a moment and when she came back, she had that war sword Jack had hung on his wall.

"Come on," she said.

Outside she handed Jack the sword, took the chicken from her mother and walked over a few feet from those stained rocks, about halfway between the house and the stables. Jack stayed where he was. He held the sword, but the whole tip of it leaned against the ground so that it looked as if he were getting ready to drop it.

22

"I said for you to come here, Jack," she said.

He moved toward her a little, a few feet, then stopped.

"Come on."

He didn't move further and neither did the rest of us. Even her mother and sister stayed in the shade of the tree. Finally Bobby and I moved, but toward the clothesline, as if maybe we were going home. But we weren't.

She watched Jack, waiting, and then she walked halfway to him. "O. K., Jack. Here." She put the chicken down. "Kill it." He just stood there. "I said kill it, Jack." She waited a moment more, then stepped up to him and slapped his face. That was the first time I had ever noticed he was as fair as she was, when the whole side of his face turned red from her hand. She slapped him again, on the other side, and when she said "Kill it," it was like she was crying. Then it didn't even look like Jack staggering with that sword through the back yard. His face was all twisted, still red from her hand, and when he swung the sword it was as if he couldn't see. He was swinging in big half circles, walking toward the chicken who was, like most chickens, stupid, but smart enough to move from something else moving near it. Still, he caught it, only a little, just enough to scare it and knock it more senseless than usual so it squawked and reeled and squawked, making more noise than it probably felt pain. Jack just dropped the sword. His mother moved quicker than I'd ever seen her do. She took a few smooth steps toward the chicken, her arm flashed out and she had it. Then, in sort of one movement, a turn toward Jack and a snapping motion of her wrist, she broke the chicken's neck and let it loose. It landed right near Jack and flopped in that way that makes you feel guilty even though you know nothing is reaching the brain anymore. Then I knew for sure Jack was crying. Bobby and I could hear it and see it. When she stepped toward Jack, I knew he backed up a little, but she kept coming and then she put her hand on his shoulder. Bobby and I went on home. I turned once to see if the chicken would keep flopping, but it was completely still.

I mentioned it at supper that night, just how she had done it, and my mother shook her head in approval as she ladled gravy; she always makes gravy. She said if someone could do it just right, it was the quickest way.

Sweet Angel Band

What was that song they had sung last night? The invitation? Annie stopped washing the pan, stared at the soap bubbles clinging to her wrists. Oh Come Angel Band, that was it. She began singing, softly at first, her fingers automatically rubbing against the bottom of the skillet for any remnants of food.

"This ain't church."

Annie stopped singing. In the edge of her vision she saw Ed switch off the television and walk straight-backed toward the kitchen. He never slumped. He was sixty-two and would never slump. She swished the skillet through the rinse water and upside down in the drainer. There. Done.

"Talk any of that gibberish tonight?"

"It's not gibberish."

"Nobody knows what they're saying."

"The Lord does." She turned her back to him and picked up the dishtowel. She was a big woman, hefty, and when she stood still as now, she settled her weight so that her legs bowed backwards, thrusting her torso upward. The pock marks on her cheeks had become deeper, darker, since she began going to church, and had lost the twenty pounds.

"Oh, the Lord, the Lord, the Lord," he said. "Should never have let you start with that business. Wouldn't have if I'd known."

"The Lord wanted me, and he would have found a way." She felt him behind her, felt his arms slide around her waist as he pushed against her.

"I want you and I got a way," he said.

"The boys'll be home any minute."

"Let's go." He stepped away, and she heard him moving toward the hallway to the bedroom. Just like that. For twenty-one years it had been "Let's go. Let's do it woman." On, grunt, grunt. Off, grunt, grunt. He had always been sixty-two. Annie untied her apron and followed him.

"I'll give you a home and a name for that baby," he had said years before. "All you got to do is give me some kids of my own. I'll treat you good. I've got a good job."

He had looked bad even then, short and squat with a jaw that stuck out as if he were saying no all the time. But his first wife had just died of cancer, and he lived in town and even if everybody knew the baby wasn't his, no one would say anything. "He's a good man," her sister would say, those nights after Ed had left, after he had shown up on the porch, like an old dog sniffing around, hat in hand, not bothering to court her, just making it seem like a fair trade. Every night he came, waiting, sometimes not talking, but eating the good dinners her sister prepared, watching television with them and from time to time looking at Annie to see if yes were coming. And Annie had lain awake nights, remembering the baby's father, how his hands would cup her breasts, just barely touching so that she must always move toward him.

So she had said yes, and now Ed sat on the bed removing his shoes. The plastic drapes brushed against the pane, a dry rasping sound that made her want to wash her hands. He had removed his clothing and his body was pale and flaccid, the flesh drooping above the joints and the skin wrinkling into flat minuscule curls.

"Well?" he said.

Annie stepped into the bathroom, turned on the faucet and moistened her hands, patting the excess onto the towel while the water continued to run. She wasn't going to wash for him. Her nightgown was on the hook behind the door. It would get soiled, but he didn't like nakedness.

Annie hurried out of Wilson's Jacket Factory a moment before the whistle sounded, before the herd of other women could punch the time clock and block up the doorway as they passed to comb their hair, apply lipstick, brush the lint from their clothing. She walked around the side of the building where the double metal doors were swinging open and the heat of the pressing room welled out as the men left in groups, laughing and joking. Ed would come out with the last, but he would expect her to be there, standing in the bare patch of yard where he could see her immediately.

"How come you suddenly got religious?" he had said two months ago and refused to let her go in spite of the fact that he knew the woman who had invited her, who was his own age, who had known his first wife. But the word had spread, by that woman and others, through the factory lines and into the pressing room, so that the men teased him, during lunch and on breaks, about being jealous even of God, and he had relented.

And now Annie did not know how she had ever lived without church. The building was small, austere, windows too high to see outside, but the heat of their bodies made it warm and the singing was all she wanted. Although she liked the other sometimes: the way one or more would suddenly rise, their mouths opening to emit a stream of words punctuated only by gasps. She would never be able to do that, but it didn't matter. They always motioned to her from the pews, indicating sit here, Annie, sit here, sing with us.

The last of the men had left the factory, and they stood beside the door, Ed among them, but he wasn't smiling, his voice not booming out with the others. He moved away before the group dispersed, walking toward her with his head down.

"Let's go home."

"I need to stop at the store."

"I ain't feeling good. Let's go home."

He told her later. "I been hurtin'. Here."

Annie felt the coolness of the sheets, their slickness. She always ironed them as his first wife had ironed them, as the doilies on the nightstand and on other furniture throughout the house were starched and ironed. She heard the front door open and one of her sons moving around in the living room, men too, both of them, one tall and dark, the other thick and short, but both happy, both hers, though one more than the other.

"You think I should see someone?"

27

"About what?"

"It hurtin' and all."

It felt strange to hear him ask her. When they were first married he had set the routine for their lives, taking care of her during her pregnancy, cooking the meals, even cleaning the house, never talking much. "He's just older," her sister said. "You get old without kids around. Besides, they say he was that way with her, too." He went with her everywhere, even shopping, and when her son was born he continued to accompany her, adamant against her wishes, so that it was easier to comply, easy to see that he was a good father. But once, when she had been laid off at work in the middle of the day, she had driven to the Cape. She never left the car, just drove and looked at the restaurant where she had worked that one year, had met her son's father. She remembered the way his shoulders had rounded down above her, how he had shrugged about the baby. Even in the car alone it embarrassed her. When she came home, Ed was waiting.

"Where you been?"

"At the Cape."

He took her wrist. He pulled her into the bedroom, and her shoulder scraped against the doorjamb before he threw her on the bed.

"What are you doing?" she screamed and pushed at his hands. He tugged at her panties, pulled them down with a sudden straight-armed bend of his body. Then he was smelling her. Smelling her.

"I can tell if you ever screw around, girl. And you won't ever do it again."

Her boy was five then. His was three. And the town had 1,032 people. She had lain on the bed, and she didn't cry.

Now he wanted to know should he see someone because he hurt. Across the hallway a door opened. It would be Lee, then, her boy, who was home.

"I don't know," she said.

Annie sang the eight days he was gone. At work she told

them of the operation, lowering her voice to say the word *prostate*. When she visited him every other night, she took her sons and they talked of the fall semester, of classes and games, not mentioning the surgery but rather how he felt, how he was coming along, and not mentioning the alternate evenings when Annie rode with a church group to Essex, to a revival there. At her machine, Annie tapped her foot while she sewed. When she stood with the church group beneath the revival tent, she saw the way sweat dotted the necks of the singers, how their hands and voices trembled with the songs.

Ed was very pale and they had not shaved him, the hairs pushing out mottled grey and black. Annie walked beside the wheelchair to the car, watched him wave aside the attendant and stand by himself, sliding into the seat and closing the door. He still looked sick. Looked old. She didn't remember his ever being sick before, ever being anything but there, grey-haired, immobile, always around her.

"Doc says I'll be good as new."

Annie slipped into the car, started the engine. "He told me you should take it easy."

"Don't have to take it easy." He settled back into the seat, watching her. His eyes were rheumy, moisture too at the corners of his mouth. "I could do it right now if I wanted. Right this minute."

"He told me it could hurt you bad." The old roadway was lined with trees, speckling the sun over the car, across the dash.

"You don't believe me, you just pull up over there."

Annie shook her head. When she looked at him, he nodded his head, sitting straighter. "Well, I could."

He had worked in the garden for the three days he had been home, against the doctor's instructions, mumbling at its condition in his absence. The garden was edged with old lumber, pieces of wood that he had placed there during his first marriage and were now dark and rotting. Annie watched him lift the lettuce head and shake it gently.

"The church group's singing over at Acorn Ridge."

He said nothing.

"Told the preacher I'd be coming."

"You're done with that." When he stood, his body retained a curve for a moment before he turned and exited the garden onto the grass toward the house. Annie followed him.

"Ain't nothing to it. Just singing."

"You ain't going."

"I already been singing with 'em."

He stopped at the steps, cradling the vegetables in the crook of his arm.

"I heard that. You think I didn't hear it? Running around the countryside while I was sick? I heard it." His hand on the screen door quivered.

"I'm going," she said.

"No you ain't."

She folded her arms beneath her breasts, tilted her head upward toward him. "I am."

"I'll tell your boy what you were," he said. "You leave this house, and I'll tell that pretty boy of yours."

Annie cooked dinner for them. The table was filled with bowls and platters, green beans, potatoes, corn, ham, lettuce and radishes from his garden. She couldn't eat. The male voices rose around the table like steam. When they moved to the television, she cleaned the kitchen, scoured the black skillet, greased it, rubbed salt in the grease, baked it solid and smooth in the oven. She could see the car driving to Acorn Ridge, see the building, the welcoming, the bowed heads, the rustling as they settled for the singing. She mopped the linoleum, moved to the doorway and looked at Ed where he sat, knees out, arms angled down so that his hands clasped at his abdomen. Then she shut herself in the bathroom. She bathed, rebraided her hair into twin coils framing her face. She didn't look in the mirror. In bed, she lay on her back, staring upward. When he came in, she pretended sleep.

"Annie."

She didn't answer. She felt his heavy arm pulling her toward him.

Ed visited the factory at the end of the week, carrying the box of produce by himself to the coffee area. From her machine Annie could hear him laughing with the men on their break, showing them how fast he healed. When the voices lowered, she knew what he was telling them, knew they would shift their eyes toward her, slap him on the back. Annie stitched pocket after pocket, never taking her own break and not looking up until she heard someone calling her name, saw a man running toward the pocket line.

"God, blood is pouring from him, Annie. He must've ripped something, that stuff he carried in, I don't know if he'll make it. Jess Wilcox says he'll drive you." All the machines stopped, the people turning as Annie ran toward the front of the building where Ed was being carried by two men.

"Annie!" he screamed when she got there, and all the way to the car, "Annie!" They put him in the back seat, and she got in with him. He half lay, his hands curling down toward his groin. The white around his eyes showed, and she had never seen that before. "Annie. My God. Annie." The car was moving, fast. Fifty miles. They wouldn't make it. The blood was seeping through his slacks, making them black to his knees. It didn't look like blood to her; it looked darker, thinner. "Annie Annie Annie Annie." A monotone, a church hymn. She emptied her purse, turned him on his side with a touch of her hand and caught the blood. "My God." He saw the liquid filling her purse. He clutched himself, turning his eyes to her with his mouth open and silent and she saw his tongue move.

Annie stood at the foot of the hospital bed. Ed lay on his back, the skin of his face drawn tight from the sloping flesh. He was sleeping, and she watched him breathe, the slight spasm of his lips as the air left. He could go home anytime, the doctor said. Anytime. The room was cool, quiet. On the nightstand were flowers the church had sent. Annie walked to the vase, touched it with her fingertips. A hum began in her throat, and she stopped it, looked toward the bed again. "We're singing at

Coleville tomorrow night," she said. For a moment she thought he answered, but he lay still. She touched his arm. "Ed. Ed." When his eyes opened, she straightened the sheet, smoothing it with her hands. "We're singing at Coleville tomorrow night."

Bootheel

Sometime in the late October night the snow had begun, covering the black soil of the Missouri Bootheel region and blowing deep against the house and trailer ten miles from Buxton. Inside the trailer Lester Carlton had slept on, occasionally waking to rub mentholatum beneath his nostrils and over his dry lips as his mother had done when he was ill as a child. Only he was no longer a child and the illness would not be passing in one or two day's time. Across from him warm air hissed from the small heater he had lighted at the first sign of cooler nights and around him the single long room was orderly–which would have surprised the people in Buxton. His few belongings in the kitchen were placed clean in the cupboards, his clothes for the morning were folded on a chair at the end of the bed and the new shotgun was leaned, unloaded, by the door, a box of shells lying near the butt. The gun had cost him all of his last Social Security check, cost him setting them up for the boys at Sandy's.

Now, still before dawn, Lester saw the snow. He stood at the window, a beer can in one hand and an unlighted cigarette in the other. "Damn," he said. "Goddamn it to hell I can't go." He couldn't see the highway beyond, or the fields, but the yellow porch light from his brother's house lit up the expanse of snow across the backyard and turned the outside dark into a murky twilight. He hated snow; hated cold; hated the way Missouri crept up on you promising warm days or dry days, then coming together in the night with something that would bitch up all your plans. If he were younger, even five years ago, he would be out on the highway, not just hitching into Sandy's, but beyond, out where the land was barren with nothing to grab and keep it close. He sipped from the beer, holding each swallow in his mouth to warm it. He could go some other day. But he had told Paddy today. That cold would rise up from the ground and hold the coat from his body. He'd be too still to pull the trigger by the time he got to the woods.

Lester finished the beer, made himself shave as he had done every morning all his life, whether in a house or in a field somewhere, having to wet his face with dew or spit. He was whitehaired and so thin that when he dressed in the jeans and shirt, ironed crisp as always, the clothing hung from his body in angles. The empty beer can he put in the black suitcase he had used to travel with, and pushed the case back beneath the bed. When it was full he would carry it down to the canal branch beyond the fields and empty it. If he threw it in the trash, Bill would have to lecture him; it was Bill's way. Lecture him and worry about him and feel sorry for him but let him do what he would. Just like Bill drove him into town once a month when the check came, saying, "You shouldn't do this, Lester. You're killing yourself." But he wouldn't stop him and he wouldn't stop taking care of him because of it.

"You bitch," he said, leaning again to the pane. The snow was thickest by the side of the house, scalloped against the black tarpaper. Only the front of the house was shingled. Biggers, who owned the place, couldn't see any reason to shingle it and Bill and Martha could never come up with enough money to shingle the rest. They'd raised four kids, all of which were okay, working at the factory at Togie or the one in Buxton, having their own kids, being Carltons, never getting anywhere. "You bitch," he said again, but he took his coat from the closet, put the cigarette in the pocket. He shouldn't go. He buttoned the coat to the neckline, then wrapped a wool scarf around his neck, pulling it across his mouth and nose.

Outside the air was still, a quiet cold. Lester pushed his hands into his pockets, holding the gun with the crook of his arm, and began walking. The snow came to mid-calf, powdery and clinging white on his jeans, then turning black into the cloth. At first he tried moving against it, pushing twin paths toward the house, but his breathing quickened immediately and he had to stop. Above him the sky was still dark but he could see the slope glistening white and smooth to the highway ahead. He hated that slope. When the rain came, the yard always filled with water so the house had been built on concrete corner blocks, without a real foundation. Bill kept wooden slats on the porch to put on the dirt roadway up the slope in bad weather. And from time to time, when Bill wasn't working for Biggers, he'd haul in some gravel but it never held. Nothing you just added on ever held. But he would make the slope when he got to it as long as Bill didn't wake first and come out as he did every morning, to check on Lester in the trailer, see if he wanted to come in the house for breakfast. Lester didn't want breakfast; he didn't want anybody doing for him.

He began walking again, slowly, raising each foot to where the snow was sparser, the drag against his body less. He'd been in snow in other places: Canada, Wyoming one year. But it wasn't as heavy. Nothing was as heavy as Missouri snow. He thought it was the trees maybe, or the black soil or how everything clung together so nothing could inch in to make it lighter. It seemed to push down from above and up from below, weighted down by rotting trees and black soil and hundreds, maybe thousands, of Carltons who had all been poor and fair-skinned and black-headed and never owned anything. Who lived in tarpaper shacks loaned them for working, who got sick and curled up uglier than other people. Carltons and Laferties like them and Turmans like them. And a Paddy Murphy who was on top of that an ass at the best of times and on top of that had only half a face, just like it had been planned on too, the way things got planned surely somewhere.

Already he could feel the slight rasping in his chest, tightness at the base of his throat. Was a time when he could have cleared the slope in seconds and laughed at Bill for staying. Now it was step, hold, brace. And he couldn't laugh anymore. And Paddy couldn't talk anymore. Had to write down what kind of gun to buy. Just lay in that bed, unable to even get to Sandy's; laying there dark-skinned and oily-haired like all his people, with nothing left him but visits from preachers and church groups and people like Lester Carlton, who had never even liked him, who had gone to see him maybe to brag a little. Maybe to not be breathing like a man should, but to still have all his body, all his face. Buying the gun from old Wilkinson's and not telling them what he was going to do with it. Probably thought he was going to kill himself. Didn't ask, though. Didn't ask.

On the crest, he rested, trying to keep his lips open only a little, to breathe warmed air. "How come you keep trying to live like you've lived?" Bill had asked. "You're old and you're sick and you keep trying to act like you're twenty-five and nothing's permanent." He was only fifty-six. Fifty-six. But his body was seventy or more and he wouldn't be hitching out of town anymore, or coming back and letting them wonder where Lester Carlton had been and what he had done this time. Now they all knew where he was and how he was. They knew he was in the trailer next to the shanty in Carlton's Hollow, below. That's what the people in Buxton called it. They liked giving names to places. Years ago it had been Togie, where a railroad line went through. His Dad had worked for the railroad a few weeks; but he got drunk and lost that job, too.

Lester wrapped his arms around his knees, pressed his lips into the rough warmth of the scarf. A car would come by soon: some factory worker making sure he clocked in on time in Buxton. He wouldn't have to wait long. Paddy's eyes had looked like a trapped bird's and they watered. But the Murphys had always had watery eyes. Watery eyes and weak looks and dirty kids and the worst shanties around.

The car finally came. Lester slipped from the roadway, waited until it passed. Then he stepped over the tire marks, used the scarf to brush in his footprints cross the road and at the beginning of the other slope. Bill would think he had caught a ride into Sandy's. He would worry a little, but worrying pleased Bill. It would make his day of loading hogs at Biggers pass quicker.

Now beneath the snow the ground was uneven, frozen raw,

but the sky had lightened. He could see the line of trees that marked off the north edge of the field. The land had been cleared to property lines, no further, and the trees were black and dense, mostly old, the young ones not getting enough light to push through and grow over waist high. He hadn't helped clear the fields; probably his granddaddy had, or beyond that even; but he had worked them at different times in his life, for the Biggers and the Welborns who owned the Bootheel land. He had gotten drunk on Saturday nights, week nights, with the Lafferties and Murphys and others like his own kind. Now he stayed in a trailer, unable to walk as far as a baby without getting winded; hiding his beer in a milk carton to cool it and his cigarettes in a Velveeta cheese box, and leaving before dawn to do what he wanted to do. He had always left in the middle of the night, catching a night rider who had to be going out of state because people in this country didn't roam in the early hours.

Each time he had come back from somewhere, he had only told them so much. Told guys in Sandy's about a bush in Arizona that was so poison a man had died from roasting a wiener on a twig. About the way they buried people in Louisiana, the tombs above ground, like drawers, and when the rent wasn't paid, they pushed you out an opening in the back into the wet spaced ground below. But the bones were all mixed. Beneath, after years, they would be cluttered together. Here, beyond Buxton, was the Greenbriar Church. His people were buried there, and others. The names on the tombstones showed what they were: Karlten, Carrolton, Carltan; Joe Lafirtay, Hogy Lafferte; Jonethen Merphie. Like no one was sure enough to have even lived.

He had to rest again, hunched down against his knees and trying not to hear the shudder of his own breathing. Sometimes it made him panic, and he didn't want to pass out here. The field stretched out white and shiny, the sun smoothing the top like sugar crust. He stared at it, willing his body to slow, slow, to get enough air through the scarf. His mother had made snow cream from snow like this. Mixed a little canned milk and sugar in it, let it freeze outside over night. She could make something out of nothing; had to all her life.

Behind him, from the direction of the house, came the sound of a motor revving and Lester watched, waiting for his brother's truck to gun onto the highway. It came up quick, and turned, not toward Bigger's place to the east, but west, toward Buxton. Bill had decided it was too bad a day, maybe, for Lester to be getting drunk. Maybe he believed he had hitched out of state again, even if it had been four years now that he had been living in that trailer scared of choking to death someplace that wasn't Missouri. Bill and Martha had borrowed the money for that trailer and he had never paid them back. Only gave them what was left from his check after he did what he wanted. He should have paid them back. He dropped his eyes to the gun. Against it his hands were blue, mottled. Pieted, his father had always said. "Pieted skin runs in the family."

He pulled himself up by the gun stock and moved on. His body still trembled and he felt the cold had seeped deep, into the bones, the way old people said it did. Ahead, the trees were no longer a black solid line. They had form, branches, a few clumps of leaves that had withstood the heavy snow. Such trees ridged all the property lines of the flatland, and in places like here, where the land just next wasn't farmed, the trees were let go, growing thick-limbed and dense. The woods were how the Murphys had lived, acting like they owned them no matter whose land it was. They used the game to supply their meat while their women did washing and housecleaning for the townspeople to buy what little else they had.

He had never liked the Murphys. They had always been loudmouthed brawlers, beating up their women and having one child after another until the woods swarmed with Murphys, dark, wiry, little bird eyes that never rested on one spot. And drinking. When Lester started, at fourteen, the year his mother died, Paddy had been long at it. He whined and weaseled around Sandy's bar, trading squirrels and possums for liquor. But then Paddy had been motherless for a long time; T.B. of the bone, they said. When she fell that time and they discovered it, she was so brittle she never got out of bed again. And the church people brought food out to them and cleaned her house for her and then spread word around town how the Murphys lived. At least some of them had.

They had come when his mother had died, too. They brought food she couldn't eat, and she smiled at them from her bed. Her teeth had loosened from the gums so long before he hadn't known when, and they separated out long and narrow, so when she smiled her lips peeled back and she was ugly. His own teeth had started that when he was forty and he had worked at a job long enough to earn the money to have them pulled. She hadn't had any money. She had starved to death in her own house with food on the table and a pain in her stomach that wouldn't let her eat. But it wasn't anybody's fault. Nobody stopped him from getting a regular job just like nobody had stopped his father from doing the same. And no one had stopped his mother from going to a doctor. She had drunk comfrey tea, camomile tea, catnip tea and made poultices. When she'd finally been forced by the pain to go to the county, they couldn't do anything. But she refused to die in the county hospital. She died in the house she'd lived in with people who were little better than strangers bringing her things she couldn't use, coming in and seeing how she lived. Old piece of linoleum on the table. The wood floor peeling where she'd tried once to put a varnish on it but the wood was still wet and it never took. An old icebox whose door had to be wired shut but there was no ice in it anyway.

He had reached the trees but he was shaking so that he couldn't step into them. He stood with both hands pressing down over the barrel opening to hold himself still. He was lightheaded. Zigzags of light were in the center of his eyes, only blackness at the sides. If he passed out, they'd say he was senile. Say old Lester Carlton turned senile, thought he was going to town and got lost. Heart got him. Emphysema, really, but heart's what done it.

He gritted his teeth, closed his eyes, waited. The last time, after a night at Sandy's, he had just blacked out and came to in the hospital, with tubes running in his arms and nose. At least he'd be whole. Not like Paddy in that rest home with no chin, no jawbone at all, holding a towel over the bottom half of his face while Lester talked to him, told him about the news in town. How Phil Laffertie had taken a beer bottle across Peach Watson's nose; how folks were saying the little BeCraft girl was pregnant, probably by her own daddy. Paddy's eyes had jumped around like always, only they looked scared now, like something cornered and too little to fight. Old Paddy Murphy, who had never had anything but family and they weren't the kind to take him home.

Lester opened his eyes, lifted the shotgun and broke it open, finally able to push the shells into the barrel. He brushed at his eyes, stepped into the woods. The air smelled of must, old leaves and decaying trees, but the ground was free of snow. Light filtered through in shatters that made him dizzy. He sank down against a tree into a cushion of leaves moist from the ground. He could no longer see the fields. He lay back his head, rested the gun across his knees. When he had been a child a man like Paddy came through. His mother had fixed soup for him. The man had worn a hat, hard, helmet-like, with a contraption fixed to it that rounded out, covering the lower part of his face. He had carried a pencil and paper notebook and a handwritten note asking for a chore in return for a meal. Lester remembered the man taking the soup out to the porch to eat it. Lester had skipped out back to sneak around and see why the man had his mouth hidden, why he had taken the soup outside. But his mother had come up behind him and tugged him all the way into the house. He asked her later, after the man had gone away. He's been cut on, she said. Half his face is gone. Then why don't he stay home? Lester had asked. Cause he's hobo. Cause it's easier for him.

Lester sat for a long time, pressed against the tree and staring into the woods. Everything seemed so long ago. He remembered walking along on railroad tracks, remembered his mother sprinkling pepper above a lantern for him to breathe and ease his cold; remembered how they set them up for him at Sandy's when he was still a boy. The woods seemed warmer than any place he had been in a long time. When he saw the squirrel, he thought he must have dozed off not to have seen it sooner. It was at the end of a scarred branch, sitting half-curled and raising its head in rapid darts to look around. Lester lifted the shotgun, sighted. Then he lowered it again. After a while a squirrel ran quickly the length of a branch a few yards away and Lester sighted and pulled the trigger. The rebound hammered into his shoulder and he thought he felt the give of bone. But it didn't matter.

He cleaned it in the woods, leaving the pelt and innards at the base of a tree. Then, again in the field, he rubbed snow over the carcass, cleansing it before heading back toward the house. It would take him at least an hour to get there. Bill would probably be back or at Biggers, helping his boss get the livestock loaded or maybe just fixing feed. The inside of the trailer would probably seem too hot, and he'd have to open the windows for a few minutes. He'd take his pills, rest for a while, wouldn't explain to Bill or Martha at all. After he felt better, in the afternoon, he'd take out a beer and a cigarette. Then he would start the stew. He had a few onions and potatoes. He'd cut the meat real fine and cook it down so he could cut it even finer. Add a little milk to soften it down more. He had a blue kettle he could carry it in. Then, later in the evening, when the Lafferties or someone were heading into town, he'd catch a ride to the rest home. They would see him standing by the side of the road with his kettle, the Missouri winter just beginning to come down on them all, and they'd be glad to give him a ride. They all knew Lester Carlton. They had known all the Carltons.

Craryville Box

By noon, almost everyone within the city limits of Craryville knew young Fred Goff had a package containing the ashes of Margaret Leonard Benson. Someone had heard the postman ask Fred if he would deliver the package as he crossed town. At first Fred had said no and had said it pretty strongly. Then, when he heard it was from the funeral home in Chicago, and was the urn with old Margaret Benson's ashes, Fred had turned in that heavy way the Goffs had when they were embarrassed and said sure, he'd run it by.

But he hadn't. During the factory break someone called Kit Benson's office and just asked the secretary if a package had been delivered and she said no, sure not, and what was it, but of course whoever called wouldn't say. You don't just say "grand-mother's ashes" over the phone. No you don't. Times don't change that much. But the package wasn't delivered then and it wasn't delivered by three p.m. either, which meant a Goff had had a Benson's ashes for at least seven hours.

Bertha Peale, sitting with a few friends and watching the last bits of wood go into the platform for the carnival stage performance, said first that she didn't like the carnival in this new park, because before, you could have the man stop the Ferris wheel when you were on top and you could see the dial of the courthouse clock. Once a year you could see it up close. Now you could only look down and then you'd just see everybody you already knew. And second, she bet that box, if it existed at all, would never be seen again. Fred Goff would just drop it off the bridge into the Castor River, and he should. In fact, she had passed his pickup as she was coming into town and it was slowing down near the bridge. Sure. He'd stop, drop that box down and watch it soak up that dirty water. Might have to drop a few rocks on it, but he'd do it. She certainly would.

But then, Bertha, said Lila Foster, no one knows for sure that

Fred's grandfather ever held a grudge against the Bensons. At least no one ever heard him say one word against them. Even the day of the auction. You know old Goff's wife died right about Thanksgiving that year, don't you? Well, she did, and the auction was held about two days after she was in the ground. She's buried not far from Fred's place now. Right up on Greenbriar Road. My daddy told me Kit's granddad made them even auction off the kids' toys. He told me that one Christmas when none of us, he said, was acting right. How old Herbert Goff just stood by the auctioneer, hands folded, and watched everyone buy his wife's things and even his kids' toys and never complained. Never said one word to anyone there. Made me cry. Made me cry then and makes me want to cry now.

Then you can drop rocks on it, too, Bertha Peale said.

In Sandy's Bar, Peach Gibson said he remembered that the woman back then, Herbert's wife, had died of T.B. That was it. And why they didn't put the carnival around the courthouse like always sure beat him. Used to be able to watch it going up and make quick trips into the bar and back out all afternoon and evening.

That's what Kit Benson wants to change. Keep the drunks up town and the families in the park. And it wasn't really T.B. It was a burn. She had had two or three babies while they lived in that little cabin old Herbert had thrown up. That was when the mill paid in script. How many of you know about script? That's something young Kit and his wife don't put in "Notes on Green County." Kit's grandpa paid in script. Couldn't be used anywhere else but the mill store and no one could get money without mortgaging something. Herbert was working for the mill in the daytime and trying to clear his own place nights. She caught fire at the cookstove. Pictures of them you've seen. Sucked her dress right up into the fire and she just run out in the street. Road, then. Mud. Anyhow, screaming, hair was just one big flame. Because my dad told me so, that's how. Or told my mother. They, or someone, jumped on her and rolled her in the street. In the mud. Fire's what killed her.

43

T.B.

But after the fire. After. T.B. ate her up then. Damn.

Can't blame that on the Benson family.

Nobody said you could. But old Goff had to pay for the doctor and help and they wouldn't take script. Meant mortgaging.

It might, Wilena Robeson said, be worth paying for a ticket to the carnival just to see Kit Benson's face and know for sure about the box. Because Kit's bound to have heard about it by then. She certainly wouldn't buy a ticket for any other reason. Never had to before. Just walked up town. Now they build a park and then rope it off so they can charge you to go in. And, if memory served right, the Bensons had put a little article in one of their Green County history things about Herbert Goff. Might be a little guilt at work there. Showed him helping build the first church.

Bensons took pictures of everything. Still do.

Looks like, though, don't it, that old man Benson could've given that family a little more time. All those kids and all. Wife dying.

Maybe the neighbors should've pitched in a little more, Wilena. Everybody give some. Course back then, nobody had anything to give maybe. Those times were hard.

Lee Murphy wiped his cafe counter and remembered for Boots Williams that that old Goff, Herbert, could really, really play. Better than that stuff the kids play on the jukebox now. Probably better than anything that'll be on stage at the carnival tonight. Could sing, too. Lordy. Sing. Why, that logging camp, back then? They kept guitars and banjos and fiddles and a piano in that store and Herbert used to play when he could. Of course, that was before his wife, Fred's grandmother, got hurt so bad and, you know, he lost everything. Heard that he could go from one of those instruments to another and play the lordy living hell out of them and keep the song going with his voice and drumming on his pants leg with his hands while he walked to the piano. Would have liked to have heard him. Part-time preacher, too. Led singings.

Those instruments, though, they was bought and paid for and furnished by Kit's granddad. Read about the entire trip, almost two hundred miles, bargaining the price down and carting the stuff back just for the people working in the mill.

Read that myself. Didn't read how they had to stay in the store, did you? Thought not. Bought them for the people all right, but wouldn't let them out of the store.

That right?

Can't really say anything bad about the Bensons, Mary Turman said as she rang up the grocery tab. They pulled this town out of nothing but mud. The streets are here because of them, and clean because of them. Got parking meters in front of the store because of them. Got a daycare center next to the factory. So they make money. They're good people. Sometimes, just sometimes, mind you, it galls a little that the young one and his wife can't remember names. And they buy their groceries at Puxico. You didn't know that, did you? Who wants to carry tales? They have them delivered by Cox's. Sometimes they come in here for bread. Milk. It takes me a little longer to add up the tab. Just couple of minutes while they wait and, you know, don't remember names.

Went to school with Fred's dad myself, up till the eighth grade. Really sad family. Used to be afraid to eat lunch near the kids from the looks on their faces. And he, old Herbert, he whipped them if he found they took from anyone or caused anyone at all any trouble.

Looks on their faces, huh?

Yeah.

Argul Felker told his wife that church fish fry or not he had to go to the opening of the carnival, because he had stopped in at the station, just for a damn minute was all, and they had a bet going that Fred would show up at the carnival with the box. Someone had seen him get out at Benson's office, stand outside the door for a few minutes and get back in the truck with the box still under his arm. Fred and his dad had helped him get his beans in last year and he was going to go watch while Fred made this harvest, and that wasn't talking stupid. She hadn't, did she really want to know, did she really want to know, ever really known the Goffs. Had she? Had she? Well then, she didn't know what it was like to have someone knock on your door and ask if you needed a package come Christmas and to just sign your name. And for months back then, Fred's daddy and the other kids and the old man had slept in a house with no roof. Couldn't even scrounge enough pieces for a roof. And he wasn't yelling. No mother, no roof, and the old man wouldn't let one soul help them.

Someone, but for the life of her she couldn't remember who, Martha Welker said, told her that when old Herbert was dying, just a few years ago, he went off his head a bit and thought he was preaching again. Said he would be quiet all day and then, with night coming on, would sing hymns so loud the others complained. And he hadn't sung in years. Quit singing, quit church, and just about quit people after his wife died. Anyhow, they had to ask Fred's dad to quiet him down. He'd bring Fred with him and they'd talk to the old man about how it was really day time and they needed to take a bit of a nap and get back out to the field. It was all so long ago, all that. People should, she thought, just let it go. Not make such a fuss.

But, you know, the Bensons have been sort of high and mighty. Of course, they've done a lot, too. They built the new wing on the parsonage, but then they got their name in metal on the front of the church, too, and that seems close to sacrilege. And why are the padded seats reserved for them? Don't know when that started, but maybe old people, with bones that don't give, ought to sit there, but a body doesn't want to be pushy. Maybe those ashes ought to be floating in the river. Get a little cold. And maybe it would be worth going to the carnival for a little while, just an hour or so, for the ceremony.

Certainly Kit knew about the box. Just look at him up there. Whiter than usual, you're right. It is not either just the lighting on the platform. And who was it seen Fred? Where in the hell was he, then? Look who's telling who to hush. When you ever turned out before? Leave her be. Not all of us are here for that. Wish all of you'd just be quiet. But he does look ill, don't he? Hey, who knows who saw Fred? Who cares. He's here. Just look at Kit. Hush. Hush. Look there. See. He's here. Lordy. Hey, listen, look there. Sit down, damn it. Look at that walk. Yeah, the Goffs walk good. You cannot either see better if it's quiet. Hush. Hush. Damn it. He said something and we missed it. Who heard it? You? Well what was it? That? Just that? Just said he took care of it for him? Then why would he put it on the stage like that? Who else heard him? Ask up front. Ask someone on the front row. Doesn't seem like enough, does it? And how come Fred didn't sit here, do you think? With us? Thought he'd sit down for sure.

Photograph of a Young Soldier

In the war, Michael had seen a soldier cut off a little girl's head in one fell swoop. He remembered that. He remembered the long stretch of black hair jerked up, the neck fragile and thin—maybe scrawny, really, but fragile that brief second before the sword sliced through the air, the neck, and stopped some place beyond, dripping blood thinned by pouring rain. No. No blood. Rain and silver sword and a little girl's head. But how could that be? The soldier gripped the hair, muddy hair now, and carried the head to a cache of rain, rinsed the mud from the face. Then he posed for a picture. Who took the picture? Michael. Was that right?

When he came home from the war, his wife was gone off and he didn't care, though he thought he should. He moved back into his old room at his folk's house, a room with a lowered ceiling of white squares that he could push up with one finger and feel the cold draft in the space between. At night he counted the squares. Forty-four.

He went back to repairing watches in his father's jewelry store. Just before lunch time, he would walk to Lucky's Cafe on the corner and watch the girls stream out of the tobacco factory across the street. One of them was red-haired like his wife had been, only much smaller, with round shoulders and a way of tilting her head even when she was paying the cashier. Her name was Oida. She wore black slippers and had tiny feet.

He asked her to the movies.

Oida had told him about the women during the war, how they worked, twisting tobacco leaves, waiting on their men, passing around photographs. Oida had a daughter, about four, with tight red curls. Oida's husband had been a drunk, and Oida still thought about him often. Michael didn't think about his wife at all. Sometimes he thought one of the women at the factory had received that photograph and Oida had described it to him.

Once he dropped by Oida's one-room apartment and she had just come from the shower down the hall. She had on a pink robe and the little girl was sleeping on a fold-down bed behind the dining table. He had kissed Oida's neck and pushed her up against the wall and pushed aside the robe. She didn't really struggle and he had barely entered her before he came.

So when she told him she was pregnant and he had to marry her, he didn't believe it was his. How could it be? That little touch? Besides, he was still married, and he didn't have money for a divorce.

Oida got the $150.00 for his divorce, though he didn't know how. They were standing on a bluff over the Mississippi, and the little girl was somewhere nearby. It was not yet evening, but already dark, and Oida was telling him they had to marry because she wasn't going to live an ugly woman, not that kind of ugly. It was raining, and he thought about just shoving her over the bluff, just putting his fingertips on her little round shoulders and punching forward from the elbows, and she'd drop, bounce maybe, tumble over and over to the water below. But then he'd have to run after the little girl, too, and grab her arm and swing her out wide, heave her floating over and down to join her mother. So he said okay, okay.

He wouldn't move from his room, though, so Oida and her daughter came to live with him. Oida slept next to him and the little girl lay on a pallet by the chest of drawers. Every morning he and his father drove Oida and the girl to a two-story house where the babysitter lived. The house had a turret, and a front porch with a swing. Oida and the girl would be standing on the front porch when he and his father drove away. Oida waited till the girl was settled, and then walked on to the factory from there.

After six weeks, he asked Oida couldn't she send the girl to live with her grandfather. He didn't want to raise another man's kid. Oida said it was her child first. Then one night he came into his room to find Oida packing. She only had one suitcase and it was open on his bed, the little girl's clothes on top of her own, all folded into squares of various sizes. The room smelled of lemon oil. All the wood in the room was shiny. He opened his closet door and his shoes were aligned, his boxes stacked on the upper shelf. When he turned to look at Oida she was watching him but dropped her gaze to the suitcase, fumbling at the latch but getting it closed. He followed her. She put the suitcase by the front door, called her daughter, and the girl ran from the kitchen. Oida looked at him. "Someone should shoot you," she said. He watched them walk toward the corner.

He forgot what Oida looked like. He remembered the pink robe and a dark blue coat and the little girl's red curls.

He spent his days repairing watches in a cone of light, his hands steady.

When his father died, he managed the shop by himself. His mother left to live with a daughter, but he kept his same room. Every work day he had lunch at Lucky's Cafe, and men and women came from the factory where they now made shoes. He never saw a woman he liked much.

Once a letter came from his son. Oida lived only fifty miles away, down in the bootheel, in one of the little factory towns. The letter was printed and the boy said he wished Michael would come see him. Michael threw it away.

II

On rainy days, Michael sometimes thought of Oida. He would see her standing on the bluff over the Mississippi, or at the door of his parents' home. Then he would remember the $150. Once he wrote a check and wrote her name on an envelope, but he didn't know her address. By the time he found it, he no longer wanted to mail the check.

One morning the rain was so heavy that the daytime looked like night. The postman tracked mud and dripped water across the dark carpet, and shuffled mail onto the glass countertop. He complained about the weather while Michael looked at an airmail envelope, the blue stripes curving around the fragile paper. The address was a UPO box. When the postman left, Michael carried the business mail into the back room and returned to working on a silver pocket watch. The tiny gears spun frantically, then stopped, spun frantically, then stopped. He removed them one by one, laid them on a velvet cloth where they were visible and could not be lost. A customer came and Michael stood behind the counter and took out each watch she wanted to see. Her coat was mottled from the rain. She bought a wristwatch with a black band and wore it from the store. When the door closed behind her, Michael picked up the envelope, held it up to the light, then opened it. It was a photograph of a tall, slender soldier, in front of a tent. He turned it over, and there was his son's name and a date a month past. He put it back in the envelope on the counter, and returned to work.

When he cleaned each tiny wheel, he found one with a break so fine it had seemed only a scratch. He had a replacement, but as he tried to reassemble the watch, his hands shook and he had to stop often. By the time the whir of the gears was constant, his arm and side ached dully. He wondered if Oida still lived at the same address. He wondered where that boy was. He wondered if Oida still wore black slippers. He couldn't remember what she looked like. The tent was green and there were trees. Where could that be?

He closed the shop early, taking the better watches from the display window and locking them in the safe. He put the airmail envelope in the safe, too, then took it out again, slipping the photograph into his palm. He couldn't see the boy's features. He held it beneath the cone light, but still the face was blurred. When he put it away again, he opened the cash box, counted out $150, then $50 more. He had heard that she remarried her first husband. He had been a drunk. Wasn't that right? Yes, a drunk.

He took the Old Cape Highway south, and the winding road turned dark immediately. The road was lined with trees and they overlapped, making a tunnel in the rain. When the road met the junction, he turned right instead of left, and then took the second gravel turnoff. Little white houses popped out of the rain into the funnel of his headlights, but the houses were new and didn't belong there. He had driven this road before. He remembered driving by three times on the same day, not long after Oida had moved out. White clothes had hung straight still on the clothesline. The sun had been still too, and heavy hot. The little girl had been sitting on the porch step.

Now the car slid a few times in the mud roadway. He thought maybe the years had worn the house dingy, blown some shingles off. He left the motor running and rolled down his window. Cold rain splashed his face, but he studied the house and the door opened as if he had thought it to, and an old woman stepped out on the porch.

The woman let him come in and said she didn't know the MacMillans, but she'd heard they once owned the place.

His son had been born somewhere in this house, but he didn't tell the woman that. The house was small, a living room with two narrow windows—one toward the porch, one toward the side where a pond was now overflowing—one kitchen, one bedroom. The woman said part of the back porch had been closed off. She used it for a pantry but the people before had used it for a bedroom.

When he tried to hurry from her steps through the rain, he slipped, and in the car had to wipe the mud from his hands against the seat. His son was named Ivan. It was his own middle name and had been his father's name. He didn't know why Oida would do that.

The rain hadn't lessened and the wind buffeted the car, but he drove steadily, past signs of little towns bridging the road, Bell City, Gravel Hill, Aquilla. At the Buxton sign he turned again. The road was dark, narrow, the yellow just barely ahead of the car. Michael was sure what his boy would have looked like, big, barrel-chested, with a deep laugh, and dark eyes. All Michael's family had looked that way.

When he found the address, he sat in front of the house for a long time. Then he shut off the motor and sat still, rain a steady ridged run over the windows. The house was lighted. Once a gust whipped so hard, the car seemed to shake and he thought he should just go home, but he opened the door a little and then pushed it the rest of the way and was in the rain, on the sidewalk, on her front porch, and knocking at the door.

He didn't think this woman was Oida. She didn't know who he was. Even when he said "I'm Michael, Oida," she didn't seem to know who he was, but she must have, since she stepped back for him to enter. She stood by a piano. He said something about not knowing she played, and then she nodded, pointing at pictures on the piano and on a bookcase across the room. She offered him coffee, he thought. She disappeared down a hallway. The room was unbearably warm. He couldn't put his legs between the sofa and coffee table, and had to stretch them to the side.

He had seen the pictures immediately, a dark-haired young man at various ages, a wide, chubby face, then thinner, somber, then in uniform, wide smile, dark eyes, thick brows, a beautiful young soldier.

Oida came back, set a tray with steaming cups on the table in front of him. She was speaking with this whispery voice about what was he doing, coming now, this night, such a night wasn't it, such a long time.

She looked puzzled, and when he said he'd come to pay her back, the debt had bothered him all these years, she shook her head. He tried to put the money in her hand, but she closed her hand into a fist and leaned sighing against the piano, her head tilted to one side. He remembered that. He put the money on the table and said he knew he really owed her much more but this much at least he had to do.

She didn't say anything for a long time. When she did look up, it wasn't at him. She said something about Ivan and pictures. She left the room again, and he studied the photographs, the youthful open face. He could hear her in the other room, opening some door, rustling, closing a door, quiet, a click.

He pushed himself up, bumping the table as he passed it toward the bookcase. He took the picture of the chubby-faced boy, stuffed it inside his coat, and opened the front door, calling even as he stepped outside that he had to go, he hadn't meant to disturb her but he didn't want her to think he hadn't remembered, hadn't been thinking about it all these years.

He ran up the slanted, cracked walk, climbed in his car, started the engine. He pulled onto the street, drove without seeing, then flipped on the wipers. The photograph slipped to his lap and he laid it on the seat next to him. A diner's neon made the rain visible lines in front of his car. He drove by a park of some kind, then up, toward the courthouse, huge and deep red, the clock atop glowing but stopped at twelve. A junction sign flashed in his headlight and he pulled on the highway, into dark for miles. A car came toward him out of the rain, turned off, the blurred twin globes becoming sweeping beams, then vanishing. He pulled to the side, lay his head in his arms against the steering wheel. Oida wanted him dead. He remembered that.

That little girl had been dead. A troop of them had found her dead by a puddle of water. No one took a picture. No one used swords in that war. They were souvenirs. Someone made them up later. The little girl had been laughing, in a black dress, her teeth white and perfect, not real at all. So the sword came clean in the rain because there had been no blood since she was already dead. Maybe there had been no war.

The car turned cool. Some car went by; he heard the shoosh of tires; then again. When he raised up, he took the photograph. The frame was black metal, a thin line of silver on the inner rim. He traced the shape of the boy's face, the eyebrows, the mouth. The boy looked like him.

He put it back on the seat. The rain had slowed, the wind stopped. He rubbed his side, watching the moving blur of the windshield.

He started the car, turned, illuminating fence and a falling barn, and drove back to Buxton, past closed stores, meters flagged red, by the post office, five houses and there it was again, white siding, hedge in front, porch, swing.

The door was still open, and in a moment Oida's shadow filled the wedge of light. He stood on the walk and called her name. He waited, but nothing happened. He stepped on the porch and waited again. He thought he heard her speak. He opened the screen door and held the photograph toward her. In a moment she took it, then extended her hand, the money crumpled in her palm.

"Keep it for the boy," he said and she dropped the bills. They fell at his feet, but he didn't pick them up. He still couldn't go, though he wanted to, and he continued holding the screen door, listening to the deceptive soft hush of the rain. He wanted to ask something about his son, or to say something, but he didn't know what. When she began to step back, he asked her to wait, just one more moment. Had Oida had blue eyes? She was wearing a robe, a pale color, with wide lapels. Her hair was short, curly in the moist air. He asked her would she just tell him what the little girl's name had been, her daughter's name. When she did, he repeated it, and she nodded. Then she closed the door. He got in the car and waited to see her remember the money, but the door didn't open again. He went back to the porch, put the bills in his pocket. He moved to his left, toward the window. He thought he might see the gun on the table, but the curtain was too thick. He said the girl's name once more as he pulled onto the Old Cape Highway. It didn't sound right.

At home, he went in his room, opened his closet, looked at the boxes on the top shelf. He took the one on top, sat down on the bed with it. A dark cord, tied in a bow, held it closed. He pushed the box aside and lay down. He studied the ceiling, eleven this way, eleven that. He untied the cord without looking at it, and felt for the top photograph, the last one put in the box. He held it up high above his face. He looked at it and closed his eyes.

The Genius of the Bottle

Once Curtis' voice was waterfall hush, so low and sweet he could croon people to sleep. At least he could me. We were drinking buddies. I liked walking the streets with Curtis, the two of us taking the whole sidewalk, people watching him. They couldn't miss him, though they could miss me. Sometimes I didn't even know my own reflection in store windows. I'd wonder who was that squat bohunk, some kind of soft Indian rock, nearly bald, close to dying and didn't care. Some mornings when I'd whip my cap off the mirror post of the dresser, it would surprise me a little, that I wasn't at least Curtis' twin. I might have been, but forty-two years ago, some witch spelled me and I fell down a gully, busting both my knees. The doctor we had wasn't much good.

In town, Curtis lived behind me, not far. I could cut through the lot behind my house, under the wild mesquite trees where wasps hummed in shadows, across the dry river bed, and up the other side and be at Curtis' trailer. He had a hound that never knew me, or pretended not to, and would go stiff and bahooing till he almost strangled on his own sound. Sometimes I felt like kicking him, or bringing a stone crashing down on his bony pointed skull, but I never did. For one thing, I move slowly. For another, Curtis liked the hound. For another, I don't kill dogs. Who knows what they'll do?

Curtis, he was a genius with cars, like I'm a genius of the bottle, or some people are geniuses of words or electricity, or hunting or raising animals or pleasing women. Just bring Curtis a car and he'd listen for something no one else could hear. He heard complaints, whines, whispers of loose wires or dry joints, and he'd soothe that metal with Curtis talk and Curtis touch, till the car gave up trying to be a dead thing and lived again for a while. Curtis didn't just get them working— barely making it like these legs of mine—he fixed them. So

Curtis always had work.

But he never had money. Curtis said if he took money, he couldn't fix cars. "How do you know that?" I said and he said "The same way I can fix cars."

Curtis had been in Vietnam. "It's a jungle, man, you know?" he'd say each time he'd talk about it. "A goddamned jungle." He'd be sitting down, elbows on his knees, big hands holding a bottle, and he'd weave from side to side, his eyes rolling up like all sorts of limbs and branches were hanging over him, catching at him, and he'd brush them aside, and say "Fuck."

I guess he shot a lot of people over there, but he only talked about two. "Damn gooks, damn Kit Carsons, didn't know what was good for them. Wouldn't eat. You think they'd eat? Shit, no, man. They'd shake their heads and just sit there, because they didn't know what it was. Wouldn't eat what they didn't know. Go ahead and starve, Gooks, old Kit Carson scouts." Then sometimes he'd stand up and aim down like he had a rifle and make a clicking noise in his throat. He'd do it twice, look at me. Then sometimes he'd laugh.

I've never seen a jungle. I don't know anybody except people like me and Curtis. Sometimes, though, I'd see those vines he was pushing away and I'd crunch down smaller even than I am and roll my eyes and whisper "Damn Gooks."

"Damn right," Curtis would say and we'd both be quiet, him thinking about it and me watching him think. He'd had to kill them, the Gooks, since they led his unit wrong.

One morning Curtis woke up in his truck, in some part of town he didn't know. He was parked in an alley, and he didn't know if the sun was coming up or going down and he couldn't remember being sober. "That scared me, you know man? I couldn't remember if I'd ever been sober. I asked my old lady and she said no. What'd you think of that? Huh?"

So he went to a place down on Main and sat in a folding chair for almost three hours. A woman there told him the waiting list was six months.

"I said in six months I'll be dead, lady, and she got me in to

57

see this dude. I meant it too. Six months."

We were in his back yard then. It was late in the day, because the side of the trailer we were on was cool. His woman was cooking meat, because I could smell it and the hound was nosing around the screen door. I felt a little like eating, but wouldn't, since I had eaten there the last few times and I had to say no soon. He was sitting on a wide wooden chair that someone had built out of scraps, so low to the ground that Curtis' knees were almost under his chin. I uncapped the bottle I had and offered it to him.

"I can't do that no more," he said, just as easy as breathing.

I held it there a moment more. Maybe I pushed it toward him a little, so he'd know I meant it.

"No," he said, "I gotta give that up, I'm not telling you to, I wouldn't do that, but I gotta find something besides a bottle. I don't want to wake up in that truck no more, you know what I mean? That truck's not going anywhere with me sleeping my life in the front seat. You have a drink if you want, you go right ahead."

He stood up as he talked, long black hair falling over his shoulders, and he stretched like we'd been talking all night. "Guess I'd better get something to eat," he said. At the step to the trailer, he pushed the hound out of the way and patted it at the same time, and went in the house. He didn't close the door, though. Curtis never closed the door until people were out of sight.

I capped the bottle. The glass was flat but thick, with that sweet juice good whiskey still half-way to the top.

"You want to eat with us?" I heard, but I said no without looking back, and headed for the mesquites.

Curtis didn't show up at any of the spots for the next few days. Someone said he was into AA, and someone else asked me if that was true. I told them they had him sitting in folding chairs and filling out papers.

When I went by Curtis' place again, the table in his kitchen was covered with books.

"Math," he said, lifting one, "English," lifting another. I counted seven books stacked on the back of the table.

"I been a fuck-up too long," he said. He just talked about the books, where he'd bought them, how much they cost, how many pages he had read. "Listen to this man," he said once, and read me a paragraph from the math book. He stumbled over the words. "Shit," he said. "I don't even know what they're asking. Do you?"

I shook my head and he laughed again. "But I will. I'm going to read this son-of-a-bitch book till I can say it in my sleep. You just wait."

Then we ate, but outside, since the table wasn't a table anymore. It looked the same, round, wooden, a black burn the size of skillet just showing under the edge of some paper, but it wasn't a table. Curtis drank coffee and talked about what he was going to do every day, study, from sunup to sundown. I had a cup of coffee with him, and watched how the sun bled into the top of the silver trailer. His woman came to the door once but didn't say anything. I left.

Next time I saw Curtis, it was at my place. I was in bed, and heard the door rattling and something saying my name. It scared me till I realized it was Curtis out in the hall.

"Hey man," he said when I opened the door. "What you doing?"

"Sleeping."

"Wanta walk? Don't want to wake up the Gooks."

I live in one room of a house with many rooms filled with people I know but don't talk to except in the halls or to borrow a beer from every now and then. There's nothing to sit on in my room but a bed, but Curtis couldn't have sat anyway. Outside, he couldn't stand still, and he couldn't even walk with every part of his body. He'd didn't really jerk or anything, but he rubbed his arms, and turned a lot, sometimes walking backwards.

"My check's gone," I said. "Haven't got anything."

"You haven't, huh? I'm not here for that anyhow. Fuck, man.

I can't sleep is all. She told me to get out, quit talking or get out."

We walked down the alley to this gutted house and sat inside with the moon and mesquite shadows. A man named Bradshaw used to lived there, but he died about ten years ago. He was Pueblo Laguna, and was a water witch, a well genius. When he walked on dry ground, people paid attention. They found him on his own doorstep, half in, half out.

Curtis smoked three of my cigarettes and gave me a quarter because that was all he had. I wouldn't take it, so it just stayed on the ground catching moonlight.

"We got this real smart dude for a teacher," Curtis said. "Man I mean a real smart dude. Got us reading about what we think." He poked his temple. "What we think, man. I read this story, this piece of writing about what goes on up here. We get all locked up and can't see things different. That's what the man said. We die walking around. He's smart."

He was sitting with his back to a window with no glass, and his hair was sort of shining in the moonlight.

"Smarter than you?" I asked.

"No way," he said at first. Then, "Yeah, maybe. Some ways."

"I'll get us a bottle," I said. "I could maybe get us a couple dollars, get some wine."

Curtis didn't say anything, so I stood up.

"Nah," he said. "Nah."

He had leaned forward so I couldn't see his face even if I had looked. I know he was moving his head because the shadow of his hair was swinging across one patch of the floor. "You coming?"

"No." His shadow waved me away. "I'm going to sit here awhile. You go on home, huh? I don't want a drink. I'm okay."

"I'll stay. Can't sleep now anyhow."

"You go on home. I mean it. I'm fine. Curtis is fine."

"Sure he is." I sat back down across from him.

After a while he stretched out on the floor, and I knew he was trying to sleep. I lay down, too, my back to the wall.

"I didn't really understand what I read," he said. Then, a while later, "Crazy gooks. Wouldn't eat it since they didn't know what it was."

He was quiet then. But his voice had been ragged, like something else was weaving into it, maybe from the mesquite, maybe from the house we were sitting in. Things don't leave.

When I woke up, Curtis was still asleep, lying on his side, hand under his cheek, mouth open. I spoke his name and he didn't answer. I put two cigarettes in the middle of the floor and when I was outside I called his name louder. "I'm going back to my place," I said.

A few months later, Curtis found government money. He said there was more money than people to take it. All he had to do was ask for it and go to school.

"Or get crippled," I said.

He didn't answer.

When Curtis says his real name, it's like wind clicking through dry leaves.

He stopped working on cars about the same time he stopped wearing baseball caps and tee shirts. I had bought this old Chrysler, pale blue and rust brown, and he sat in the front seat most of one afternoon, listening to the engine, then burying his head and arms under the hood, then coming back to the front seat to listen again. I left it with him for a couple of days, and when I came back, he said "I done everything I can do unless I pull out the engine and sort of start all over."

"Do it then."

"I can't. I'd like to, but I can't unless you can just leave it here." We were in his trailer. He had a typewriter by the papers on what used to be the kitchen table and he said he was writing a book about Vietnam. The teacher was going to help him. "He says I'm real smart," Curtis said. "He says it's because I'm older than most of the others and because I want it worse. And he's got it, man. I want it."

He never did fix the car. I went back a week later, and he had washed it, cleaned the engine, put in a new water pump, radiator hose and cap.

"You can't figure out what's wrong with it?"

"I'm gonna rebuild the carburetor, but I don't think that's the problem."

"You can't fix it?"

"It's dead. Gone forever. Think it died before you bought it. I got it too late." He didn't look at me and I told him to forget the carburetor.

He sat in his low chair and we looked at the car and the gully and the dog. A book was open on the ground next to his chair, but he never picked it up. He said his old lady was going to move out. "She don't like me sober," he said. "They told me that's what happens. You change and everybody around you gets scared to death. You scared?"

I told him no.

I drove the car home, and when it stalled I cursed Curtis. Someone told me Curtis could have fixed the car if he'd wanted. I sold it the next week, when my check money ran out.

After that I started watching Curtis' house from the mesquite grove, only at night when I was ready to fall asleep and my room was closing in on me or my neighbors' voices were coming in like water. I'd sit near the river bed, lean against the base of a trunk, and watch the stars white cold and far away. Sometimes Curtis didn't come home before I slept, and I'd wake to know he had slipped in during the night. Sometimes he came and I'd hear their voices sharp inside the metal and out he'd come, talking to himself and slamming the car door, gunning the engine. Once I just went over and threatened the hound quiet, and asked the woman where Curtis was. She said she didn't know where he was and she didn't give a damn.

I thought he was drinking, only not willing to let me know.

It took me seven days to figure out where he went. I had to do it a street at a time, watching where he'd turn and being there the next evening. Sometime I just stayed where I was and thought about Curtis drinking alone. I'd point my finger at a face on some sign and say bang.

I took a bus part way and then walked. People drove by and they pulled clear, away from a twisted fat pork Indian hobbling drunk up the mountain. There's only one road up A Mountain from our side of town, but many little ruts lead out from the main road. I didn't know where Curtis had gone. I sat on a rock at Gates Pass and could see the entire town below, the sky turned upside down, all night-silent. I had to stop breathing to hear some wind and bird, and once a coyote, but I never heard Curtis.

So I went up there early the next night, and watched until a car branched off from the main road. Then I walked down the hill and took the same path. The moon was up, but couldn't do much because the trees had walled off the road. I found his car, just stopped in the ruts, empty. I sat on the hood, and after a while I heard this high thin moan, like something pretending to be wind in the trees.

When it stopped, I got off the car and tried to hurry down the road, but I fell. I just rolled a little and lay still. I could see Curtis coming around the car. He was big and loose, with his hair gone or skinned back. He had no shirt and he looked white against the dark in spite of the moon. When he was gone, I tried walking out, but finally I sat in the middle of the road until morning so I could see where I was going. Once I started to sleep, but this net dropped down and I saw it coming and stayed awake.

Curtis left not long after that night, and the trailer just sits there empty.

A few weeks ago a man named Curtis came by my place. He wanted to take me to dinner but I told him no. He wanted to give me some money, but I said no to that, too. "You could at least talk to me," he said, so I put on my cap and followed him outside. We walked by the gutted out house, the front door gone, shadows and the last of the sunlight shifting on the dirt floor.

"That was a bad night," the man said.

I said yes it was, but I didn't look at him. He talked some

more, but he finally gave up and went away.

Curtis must have taken his dog with him, because no matter where I walk, no dog goes stiff and bahoos at me. Now I go up the mountain and into the trees at night. I've put three tin plates on a flat stone I found. I build a fire. Sometimes I drink. Sometimes I talk. I crouch down and speak very softly, trying to hush talk Curtis back out.

Painting

Cora knew that if it had been her mother's decision to kill the dog—and to kill the dog was the exact question being posed— her mother would have simply painted the kitchen some intrusive color during the middle of the night, and in the morning, of course the dog could live, blind dog or not, dripping hairs like an overgrown dandelion, making semi-gelled puddles, at least semi-gelled by the time Cora arrived home. It could live. The hours of labor while the world slept would have eased the need to act, either physically or emotionally, and the enveloping of a new strange color in the familiar kitchen would, besides, envelop the question of the dog.

But in the long run, Cora knew, the decisions were about the same: to paint or to kill. Now, from the corner of the sofa, which was hairy from the hair of the dog before her, a dog lying by the rung of the rocker which, if Cora were to sit in, the dog would trust her not to rock, now Cora could see the dog waiting. Whenever decision time came around, the dog waited. Usually the dog was called Lady, but not today. Today it had to be an object just exactly the same as halls or hallways that were painted in the middle of the night. Or once, once, an entire metal cupboard, painted a color of green that comes only by the mixing of two shades and brands made ten years ago and watered down with a shade of yellow thrown in, the yellow of the hallway a year or two before.

But in her mother's time, which might still be presently occurring but not the same time as her own, Cora decided, paint and walls held things together. Dogs were kept for children, and homes were kept for children, and husbands were kept and children were kept. And things, Cora supposed, such as dignity and principles were attained by hanging orange-striped potholders on green plaid wallpaper pasted behind the stove because "you can't worry about little things like clashes," her mother would say.

"And of course you can't kill the dog," she would also say, if she were asked, which she wasn't going to be. Some things one didn't say to mothers who were miles away and sixty years old; perhaps, under new time, older. This mother, for example, had pauses that came after statements, pauses that could remain in one's ear for weeks, even wake one up slightly at night to hope the next word had come, and that it had been a kinder word. "I'm getting a divorce, Momma." Pause. And for a long time. "Say something, please." And then, after awhile, the pause would give way to little, little words that sounded like "I can't think of anything to say." After which, Cora was sure, the living room got painted.

But of course the dog, that dog, beneath the rocker, was quite old and no one could expect hesitation or doubt, unless they knew about the doubt already. Then it was wrong. "Are you sure?" from counselors and friends. But, Cora had learned, don't say "no." Instead say that all your experience and all your inner desires point in the same direction. But in the middle of the night, who could be sure about the color of paint in the daytime? Besides, in addition to being blind, the dog ran toward the slightest draft as if light certainly lay beyond and blindness had just settled on her because she had been in the wrong corner. At the least bit of chink, of space, she was gone, running down the middle of the street, willing to die by accident for something that didn't exist.

Certainly, Cora knew, she, too, was trying to see, spending days, weeks and months craning backward and forward and sideways in time, peering into the eyes of strangers and friends, examining words, and settling, finally, on the dog. Then she really could be sure. Because if one could leave children, could sit on their beds the same day they were preparing to leave for college, if one could do that, with trees outside shading the bedroom window, and suitcases open on the floor, and one could not wait so badly that she just blurted out how she was leaving and how first years away from home were not easy even if the home were still there, well, if one could do that, one could certainly have a blind dog killed; and should. Otherwise, little rules kept bleeding through like paint.

And, besides, there weren't any rules at all unless one made them, arbitrarily, to fit everything in. She, for example, could say, "The perimeter of Cora is. . ." and fill the spaces and look at it from time to time to know who she was. Then, if everything didn't fit within that perimeter then she, Cora, no longer existed. Or she had to change the perimeter. Now, within these four lines is: someone who spends whole nights on the sofa; someone who thought permanent meant from here to a gravestone and discovered the gravestone before the end; someone who lived in a world where, if one trusted magazines in doctors' offices, they had discovered that in the seventh mathematical dimension there were four kinds of spheres. If she lived forty more years, Cora knew, a globe would be a globe. They had moved past the third dimension through the fourth, fifth and sixth, and everyone was in the seventh. Except her. And, of course, her mother.

Then one had to be able to kill a dog if one wanted to stay in any dimension at all. She could kill a dog. She could call her mother and say, "I'm going to have the dog put to sleep." Or maybe say "I killed Lady. It needed to be done and I just did it." Then, when the silence was speaking for her mother, she could add a few things to keep the direction right. She could tell her it was foolish to think clashes didn't matter; that homemade upholstery was pathetic as were homemade clothes and orange kitchens and mothers who painted all night and then smiled in the mornings and who said "of a night" instead of "at night" and "had went to the doctor" instead of "had gone to the doctor," and who, even if she spoke French, would say things the same way. The world was in neutral colors now and if you had too much color you were, Cora was sorry, crazy. You had to learn to blend everything; a man, for example, who asked you to please time it right, and just at that moment, the exact moment, would you please slip down and catch it in your mouth? Or another who suddenly slipped up on your body and held your arms while he gagged you with himself and then lay wrapped around you and talked about how wonderful it had been. To which the right reply was? What a furious paint job, Mother, that would have been. One had to blend those women; the one who said yes and the one who thought no.

One of those women could kill a dog. And if one could do it, personally, particularly personally, if one could do it and look at it and say yes, that is just what it is, it is red all over my hands, then maybe one could accept it. With a hammer or knife in one's own hands, but right there, looking at it dissolve everything you knew about you, and then get up and live through the next day, it would be better. It would not matter whether or not the walls of the kitchen met, because people spoke more languages than anyone could learn in one lifetime, even one straight lifetime. Because once ever so many years something blocked out the light of some star they were watching, and if they couldn't determine what it was—and they haven't been able to so far—then how the hell did they know the star was behind it, just then, at that moment? The walls might not be there, Mother. Only the paint. What do you think of that?

Then one wouldn't have to understand mothers. Or be one. Or sit awake and think of that small woman in that small kitchen or the lines in the face before the painting. Or how children couldn't understand anyhow, and it was no wonder, because who could? Even years later, time later. They made quick little remarks, tight words from tight-pressed, prim little mouths that had sucked breasts and bitten fingers and drawn on new paint and made silences in mothers. They asked their fathers for things like the china teapot or the book with the silver on the blue cover. And they loved dogs and fathers, and talking about right and wrong as if the meanings were as firm as the rows of the letters. And they would, perhaps, someday, sit for long, long hours on the corner of the sofa, waiting for the night to pass and hoping there was, and they could find, a difference in killing the dog and painting the kitchen.

Cora's Room

"Maybe God will paralyze my other vocal cord so you won't have to hear my voice," Oida whispered from the doorway.

Cora curled on her side in the bed, put her hands over her face.

"Everyone else has got me," Oida said, "and now you've done it, too."

Cora heard her mother walking away, stopping in the center of the living room. She would be standing with head down, staring at the floor, one wrist upturned at her waist, as she had taught Cora to stand. In a moment, Cora heard the soft, raspy voice again. "I wish I was dead."

Cora kept her hands over her face. Why had she stayed here this long? Why hadn't she better control over her own mouth, her expressions? "I'm boring you, aren't I, honey," her mother would say. "It's just that I haven't seen you in so long, and there's so much to say." And off she would putter, to the kitchen stove, where she cooked incessantly for Cora, who did not wish to eat, and wasn't sure, lately, that she wanted to stay alive. Homes were places for nourishment, she had believed, but thus far the nourishment had been breakfasts before she had smoked enough to quieten her mouth, or had drunk enough coffee to open her eyes. Lunches at eleven-thirty, at the table, places set, ice water, napkins. And now. Lord. She had hurt her mother.

She sat up. She had always loved this place, and her mother. At one time this room had been pink, then yellow. Now it was wallpapered in white, with pastel green, minute bridges over unseen water, being crossed by tiny women with parasols. Her mother had hung this paper before Cora's last trip home, four years ago, at the time of the divorce. This trip had resulted in a new porch for the front of the house, and a fake-wood partition to separate the kitchen table from the stove. "I know you're used to nice things, honey. This place is old, but I try, you know, to keep it looking good."

Yes, Cora knew. She swung her legs over the edge of the bed and brushed back her hair, seeing herself in the dresser mirror beyond. The woman looking back would soon be the type they used to show in anti-smoking demonstrations: "Do you want to look like this in the morning?" No, she didn't. But here she was, over forty. And her mother said she would probably line fast, being so fair, like her father, and should try the vanishing cream Oida had always used. Now she wondered if she, Cora, were as hard on the inside as she looked on the outside. She made herself stand up and take a few steps toward the living room, listening. There were no sobs. Maybe that was worse. She padded down the hallway.

"Mother?" The door eased open, stuck against the linoleum. "Mother?"

Oida was sitting up, pillows stacked behind her. She turned her face aside. Cora sat on the bed. "I'm so, so sorry," she said. "I didn't mean it, Momma." She laid her head against Oida's breasts. "I just got beside myself, you know? The things you talk about are so sad. I want to stop them, go back and erase them, make your life happy. And I can't." She heard the sigh coming, then felt the light stroking of her hair. In a moment, she sat up. Her mother's hands were still moving slightly, picking at the nightgown. Against the pink satin, and in the shadowed bedroom, they looked as delicate as those of a young girl. Cora looked at her own, larger, stronger. "I'm really, really sorry."

"I guess we don't know each other anymore, honey," Oida said. "We don't spend enough time together. Kids move away. They change."

"I haven't changed. I just can't think of you being hurt. Sick."

"But I *was* hurt. Your father hurt me. My own brothers and sisters hurt me. You want me to act like I wasn't hurt?"

"No. No. I just can't fix it. Talking about it makes it happen again."

From the kitchen came the deep hum of the refrigerator.

Cora could feel the vibration in the floor.

"Well," Oida said, and sighed, pressing backward against the pillows. "What's done is done. We'll have to learn to talk to each other."

"I'm sorry, Momma."

In her room again, Cora lay flat on her back, legs bent. She had opened the window, in spite of the danger of "night air too wet to sleep under," and could hear the cicadas in the yard. Out there, on the old porch, was where she used to sit and dream of waltzing on polished floors, of speaking fluently at least ten languages. She still owned at least fifteen dictionaries and could say hello and goodbye in each language. And I love you. She rubbed her fingertips against the cool sheets. But that was past. Fairytales and futures.

Cora woke early, dressed without showering. She eased out the front door, taking her cigarettes, and carried the lawn chairs to the back yard, under the elm tree. The cuffs of her jeans were damp, bits of grass clinging to them. She smoked, propping her bare feet against one of the chairs. She heard the back door, saw Oida stopping at the hollyhock, breaking off some leaves. Her back was so rounded that it pulled up her housedress, and a wide strip of the slip lace showed beneath. Even in the summer, her mother would wear a slip.

"I'm still sorry, Mother," Cora called.

Her mother walked down the sloping yard toward the garden. "I'll have breakfast ready in a few minutes," she said, stooping over the first row. "Want to check these tomatoes."

"I don't want any breakfast." Cora leaned over the side of the chair, picked up the butts and started toward the house.

"You need to eat, though," she heard from behind, and could still hear a soft buzz when she reached the back steps. Her mother would talk even if she heard the car motor start. Cora ran water on the cigarettes, dropped them in the trash can by the back door, then sprayed Lysol to cover the odor.

"That white butterfly out there," Oida came through the door with three tomatoes in her hand, "wants to lay eggs on my broccoli." She put the tomatoes on the freezer and took a jar of white powder from the curtained utility cabinet. "I'll just put some of this out right now." She tapped the jar. Cora poured a cup of coffee and stood at the kitchen window, watching Oida dust powder in the garden beyond. As long as she could remember, her mother had never stopped working; and now, never stopped talking.

Cora sat down at the table. She could leave today, be in D. C. by tomorrow afternoon. With Jack by tomorrow night.

"I've got the fruit already cut," Oida said as she entered the kitchen, "and the eggs will only take a minute." She washed her hands at the sink and opened the refrigerator. "That old Bill Wilhelm," she nodded her head toward the back yard, and, Cora supposed, the house on the other side, "is in the Sikeston hospital." She carried the eggs to the counter. "Went there for heart trouble, but they found a spot on his lung, too." She glanced at Cora and stopped talking for a moment.

"I wasn't telling it to you," she said, and cracked the eggs into the bowl. "I would have been talking about it even if you weren't here."

"It's okay."

"It's living alone that does it. Since I retired from the factory. Which I should have done long ago, you know, when Dr. Falls told me about the scoliosis and the arthritis and, remember how my hands used to go numb? Right here?" She turned toward the table, then jerked back. She whipped the eggs, speaking in little mutters to the stove burner, the skillet, the butter. "People don't know what it's like. . . being sick. . . years and years. . . 'Nothing's wrong with you, Oida, except you're depressed.' Depressed, huh. Working for children so they won't do without in spite of a. . . "

"I'm going outside, Momma."

Cora scooted back the chair, walked through the laundry room and tried to shut the screen door gently. She didn't want it to happen again, what happened last night. "You make me sick," she had said, had screamed it from the center of the bed, with both her hands pulling at her hair as if she would bald herself. "I've got to get the hell out of here before you drive me as crazy as you."

Her mother carried the tray casually, balancing it against her hip and stopping to look at her rose bush and baby pecan tree while she walked toward Cora. "Thought you might be hungry if you could smell the food," she said.

Cora took the tray. "I may leave today, Mother. In an hour or two."

"No." Oida sat down, folded her hands in her lap. "I mean, you don't want to go yet." She patted Cora's knee. "I don't know why you want to go there anyhow."

"I've never been anywhere."

"I know. I know. But a woman alone."

"It's only a day and a half away. Then I'll meet my friend. . . "

"There's that butterfly again." Oida pointed toward the broccoli.

". . . who has helped me a lot. . ."

"I may have to go get that powder again."

". . . and who at least is not a drunk."

Oida stopped fidgeting. "Don't talk to me that way. You've gotten real hateful, Cora. Real hard."

"You don't listen to me."

"I listen to you."

"No." Cora put the tray on the ground between them, the eggs still steaming a little, orange pulp clinging to the glass, everything as it was when Oida carried it out. "You don't even ask me any questions, Momma."

"I know you work hard, honey. So did I. I used to wonder how. . . "

"And I live with this man named Jack. Or did until. . . "

Oida picked up the tray and hurried toward the back door.

"Jack Murphy, who is more than ten years younger than I and. . . "

Cora bent forward, hugging her knees. She used to feel wonderful in this back yard. She raised her head and looked

73

toward the house, at the bottom of the kitchen window, where the window fan had begun its whir, meaning Oida felt too warm. "You're so fine," her mother had always said. And "This is my daughter, Cora. The one in Arizona. She teaches." Her mother had been petite, redhaired, gentle. Now the fair skin was crepey, and jowls quivered beneath her cheeks. She read obituaries and called the funeral home to see if the Phil Wilton they had for viewing was the Phil Wilton from Dexter.

Cora walked around the side of the house, going in the front door and into her bedroom. She took her suitcase from the closet and opened it quietly. She slipped open the dresser drawer, began lifting out the soft silk undergarments. Her mother was already coming up the hall.

Oida gripped the bed post. "You're not really leaving. Not now?"

"I'm making you unhappy."

"Oh no, you're not. We haven't even had a good visit. I just," she clasped her hands beneath her breasts, "I just can't talk about some things."

Cora removed the few hangers with her clothing. "Neither can I."

"But we could talk about other things."

"What other things?"

"We could talk about when you get married again."

"You may have only one vocal cord, but it's a big one."

"Your father used to talk to me that way."

"I know. I'm sorry."

Oida started to refold the shirts Cora had laid by the suitcase, then stopped. "Guess you know how you want these." She sat in the chair near the bed. "Did you like that vanishing cream?"

"It's a little drying."

"But it smoothes lines. You can add a little lotion afterwards." Oida stood up. "I'll get it for you."

"I can pick some up."

"I've got an extra jar somewhere. I bought it just in case, you know, they quit making it. I've used it for years."

She came back in a moment, a little breathless. "Here, I got your stuff." She laid them on the bed, a jar of vanishing cream, Cora's makeup bag, a toothbrush, two wash cloths. "You can always use washcloths."

"Thanks. Well." Cora glanced around her, toward Oida and then away. "I guess I'll make a run through the house."

"Let me fix some sandwiches."

"No."

They walked through the house together. In the kitchen, Oida opened the refrigerator and reached for a bag of apples, then closed the door without taking them out. Cora gathered up the ashtrays and washed them in the bathroom sink, then put them in the utility cabinet. Oida leaned against the stove. "Can I fill the thermos?"

"That's all right. I'll stop for coffee up the road."Cora touched her mother's hair briefly. "When do you see Doctor. . . Halls again?"

"Falls. Dr. Falls. Two months. Just a checkup." She waved it away.

"He's a good doctor, I guess."

Oida nodded. "But, you know, there's nothing really wrong with me. Just need checkups."

"Can't be too careful. Be sure and go."

"I will."

They walked outside. Cora put the suitcase in the trunk. Oida stood by the car door.

"You drive real careful, hon."

"I will. I made it this far."

"I know. I just worry. Things have changed so. Highways aren't safe."

"You going to work in the garden?"

"I might." Oida looked toward the house. "You're just leaving so fast."

"I've been here a week. I've seen everyone."

Oida put her hand on the door window frame. Cora covered it with her own.

"You have deadlines, though, I guess," Oida said.

Cora shook her head yes, started the car.

"When's he gonna be there? That. . . Jack?"

"Tomorrow night."

"Well. You drive careful." Oida stepped back. "The new porch looks good, doesn't it?"

"Yes. The whole place looks good. You take care of it well."

"I'm retired. I've got the time."

"I'll call you from D. C."

"No. Okay. Do that."

Cora drove away. In the mirror she could see her mother standing on the sidewalk, looking after the car. She wanted to drive back, but she kept going. Her mother would strip the bed and put on clean sheets. Then she would close the window Cora had opened and push back the curtains so that light flooded the room. She would stand with her head down, maybe one hand on the bed post. She would sigh. In the soft cast of the room, the green from the plants outside and the bits of green in the wallpaper, she would look younger, her short hair still curly, the lines of her arms and hands lovely. Cora kept driving.

Witches

Bluebird and Cora were going with the play to Phoenix. Bluebird loved it. The idea alone was like a fragile bubble too delicate even to examine, much less with critical eyes, as Bluebird knew hers were. She'd chew it, inhale it. Burp it out grotesque and ugly.

Bluebird knew her world vision was black.

Bluebird hated Cora; Bluebird loved Cora.

Cora had protested at the group's tryout, and still protested, that she couldn't do it. "I can't read music," she said. "I can't do those rhythms, and I'm too old to try."

"Learn, damn it." That had been the first time Bluebird had ever, ever, spoken harshly—commandingly—to Cora, and it had worked. Cora continued to teach and attend classes, but the rest of the week, when she wasn't at rehearsals, she practiced reading sheet music. The only solo lead she had to do was a jig, six bars of a jig. But it was an odd tune, the frenetic drive of the fiddle and mandolin ceasing suddenly, then the guitar beginning, slowly, mournfully, as if the melody had to grow to speed. Cora had worked so hard to learn the dropped rhythm, that she had to sleep with a heating pad wrapped around her forearm.

"I'm the worst in the group," she still said, though, which Bluebird conceded was right: Cora would never be a good musician, and the brilliance of her timing was in life, in positioning, not in music. It was that Cora said "I can't" at the precise point someone needed her to be able to do something, and then, when the pinch came, outperformed herself, for brief encapsulated moments playing far above her own ability, as if she transformed desire into talent. Just for moments, however. She couldn't be relied on like the others, Betty or even Grace, and certainly not like Bluebird. Yet people gave way to Cora, to tiny, blue-eyed, red-haired, square-shouldered Cora Leban, while Cora simply protested her way through the admiring crowd.

Bluebird opened her eyes, stared at the ceiling, kept her body relaxed. Gradually, concentrating on the muscles from her toes up, she tightened, tightened, till she felt herself a wire against the mattress. She stared at the prisms hanging from the ceiling fixture, blue, purple, angles, darts. She took a deep breath, went limp, began again.

She had told Cora once that she, Bluebird, could almost climax just from exercising.

"Really? Cora had said.

Bluebird had dropped the subject. The world was so straight for Cora.

Cora Leban was a little afraid of Bluebird Willey, and not for any concrete fact. So Bluebird saw a counselor—so had Cora, and for years. She liked, for a while, Bluebird's posturing, her quick turns, her deliberate, dramatic poses. "Friendliness," Bluebird would say, and her eyes would become softer, as if a deeper blue; her hands would be loose. "Hate," Bluebird would say, and the eyes would pale, the hands appear thinner, flattened. Once, with eyes glazed, mouth sweetly curved, head tilted in the most childlike way, Bluebird had said "Filth, slime, suck, succubus, scuz cunt," and Cora had felt as if she had been hit deep behind her eyes. Then Bluebird had laughed. "You can't trust surface, Cora. You'll never learn." She had bummed a cigarette, poured coffee, and within a few moments she was crying, and Cora was sitting next to her on the sofa, arms around her but trembling. "I hate myself," Bluebird had whispered, child voice again.

Cora had known Bluebird for six months now, and thought her the most honest, uncomfortably honest, woman Cora had known. But Cora didn't think anyone should be afraid of truth; she listened anytime Bluebird wanted to talk.

"I was abused as a child," Bluebird had said. She waited weeks to add, "not physically."

One afternoon, late, when Bluebird had left Cora's house,

Cora had been so exhausted, she was shaky. She had lain on the sofa in the den, not knowing she fell asleep, believing that the gray mist in the room was actually there, thickening, swirling slower and slower till suddenly, from the sofa, as if from Cora herself, had risen this solid black form, first elongating itself as a leech in water, becoming hard, black, crowned with a pointed hat, beneath which thick blonde hair grew in jutting spurts, and there, before Cora could fully wake, was a distorted Bluebird witch to which Cora had somehow given birth.

Cora didn't want to share rooms with Bluebird in Phoenix.

* * *

"You know, Bluebird," Cora said, but keeping her eyes on the line dividing the highway, "you haven't been acting exactly friendly in a long time. Since the play started."

"How so?"

"You know," Cora said, "as well as I do."

Bluebird shrugged. "You get embarrassing. You can tune and count as well as anyone. You don't need help."

"I don't feel sure. I'm an amateur."

"You don't have to cling." Bluebird met Cora's look, then punched the lighter in, reached for Cora's cigarettes. "Mind?"

Cora didn't answer.

"You do?" Bluebird said. "Cora? Spit it out."

"Well, yes, I do. I may cling, but you bum. Cigarettes, lunches, rides, help moving."

"Ooooh. Out it comes. You said if I needed help packing to just ask."

"Not exactly. You said you needed help and I said I had a lot of work to do, but if you couldn't get done in time, to call."

"I couldn't get done in time."

"You went out three nights in a row."

"Okay." Bluebird slipped the cigarette back in the pack.

"Smoke the goddamned thing, Bluebird."

"No thanks. I just quit."

"Smoke it. You're dramatizing."

Bluebird stared at the highway, sitting easily, casually, as far as Cora could tell.

Bluebird pretended she was a ribbon. Since the windows were open, the whipped air lifting the top layer of Cora's hair into a fine red spray, Bluebird was the ribbon streaming from Cora's hair, light, easy, delicate. She streamed over the top of the car, forward, along the road before them, then curled up, high, back, doubling, looping, into Cora's window, sliding across Cora's shoulder, resting, coming to lie at Cora's throat.

"I'm sorry," Bluebird said, and reached again for the cigarette, lighting it quickly, drawing against the coil before it had heated fully. "It's just that, sometimes, when you sort of cringe and wait for someone to say, 'you did fine, Cora, you did fine,' sometimes—those times—I don't like you at all."

Cora nodded, then drove in silence for a while, turning once to meet Bluebird's gaze and nod again. "I've wondered lately if you've ever liked me."

"I've wondered the same about you."

"Odd birds, aren't we?" Cora said.

"Yeah." Bluebird tossed the cigarette out the window. "Last one," she smiled. "Promise." Then she lay back and closed her eyes.

When Bluebird was happy, even angry, Cora found her lovely—tall, slender, vibrant, blue eyes alert and clear, her profile and cheekbones like quick sepia stills. Cora, visually, would have put a curved, wide-brimmed hat on Bluebird, pushing the thick hair up beneath the hat, slipping a sweeping white dress on the long frame, a basket over one beautiful arm, and a dark, intelligent, wonderful man at her side. Bluebird was a true, true artist, Cora knew. Music, dance, art, drama—Bluebird excelled at them all. But not at people.

"They're all pricks," Bluebird had said. "All of them. Scuz butts."

"Are you gay, Bluebird?"

"No. But I may have to be if I keep meeting assholes."

Cora had not known that being gay could be an option, like studying music.

Now, the grade steepening, the car sluggish, and Bluebird obviously deep in a dream, Cora glanced at Bluebird and continued glancing at her: chewed, bulby nails, oily hair, open mouth, the genuine sway of a knee uncontrolled in sleep. It was one of the bad phases Bluebird had talked about, Cora supposed. So Cora, by the last lonely span before the city, wanted the two of them to stay friends. People didn't have to be alike to like each other.

Bluebird, through the slitted view between lashes and cheekbones, saw Cora relax. She wanted to tell Cora that anger, if swallowed, if buried in the belly, rotted out, out, out, and emerged cringing. Putrid. Leprous. Old. Like Cora. Bluebird wanted to say that aloud.

In Phoenix, Bluebird and Cora understood why the others were actresses. They couldn't have understood in Tucson. There, the two had gone home from the theatre, Cora to her tiny house, Bluebird to her one-room apartment. In the hours at the theatre, they had practiced, performed, studied when they could; they had attended classes. They had not known that, given per diem, given time, one could rest, lie around pools, tan, call room service, browse clothing stores, spend hours before a mirror.

"They like you," Bluebird said, when they sat in their hotel room, Cora in the center of the big bed, Bluebird on the cot against the wall.

"I like them, too," Cora said. "Look, please take the big bed a while. I don't want to feel guilty."

"I want the cot, Cora. I chose it. It and the table. You can sit in the center of the bed and practice, and I can sketch."

"Practice that stupid jig. It should be in my fingerbones by now."

"You worry too much about it. You have to give in to it."

"I've tried. Over and over and over. You, Bluebird, can give in to it. I have to find it."

"When they asked you to dinner, did they say me, too?"

"You're my roommate. They were asking us both."

"Did they say it, Cora? In words?"

"Yes."

"You're lying."

"Fuck you, Bluebird."

"Debby asked Betty and Grace. Personally. They said so."

"Okay. Okay."

In a little while, Cora went after Bluebird, and found her in the back booth of the cafeteria, pencils and pad pushed aside for a plate of frenchfries.

"Look, for $15.00 more a day, we can move ground level and have twin beds."

Bluebird raised her right arm slowly, toward Cora, index finger pointing, then swept the direction past Cora and toward the lobby. "Do it, Cora, for God's sake," she said, then dropped her arm and gathered up her things. "Gotta buy some cigarettes," she said, and kissed Cora on the cheek as she passed her. "Now you'll worry about that, won't you?"

Bluebird loved being on stage, even behind the thin brown gauze curtain; especially behind the curtain. It made the performance whole, separate, softening the stage action, the audience, and keeping her and Cora, and the others, dim shadows for the people filling the seats. Bluebird watched the actresses begin filing in, the lights moving, the time arriving for the drive of Grace's fiddle, the bursting notes from Bluebird's mandolin, then the brief silence. The actresses would fall to their knees, and then would come the slow jig from Cora's guitar. Bluebird kept her hand poised over the strings, but turned her head slightly to see Cora, who was counting time, her lower lip pulled beneath white teeth, her face pale in the shadowy light. "You can do it," Bluebird whispered and smiled quickly when Cora raised her eyes. Bluebird dropped her hand over the strings, flew into the jig.

Cora tried to slam the door to their room, but the airhinge held it back. She slipped her guitar case under the bed, and began unbuttoning the long row of buttons that began at her neck and continued to and around the hem, almost brushing the floor. When Bluebird came in, Cora wouldn't look at her, and moved away when she felt Bluebird standing behind her.

"Cora."

Cora unfastened her hair, turned and sat on her bed. "What?"

"Don't worry about it. Nobody noticed."

"You noticed. Or you wouldn't be saying this."

"I know how it's supposed to sound. They don't."

"God." Cora rubbed her eyes, shook her head, pulled her hair over her shoulders and began braiding it. "I feel like going back home."

"They like you, everyone of them."

"Sure."

"They say you look like an authentic mountain woman."

"Great tribute to a guitar player behind a curtain."

"Okay. Have it your way. You were lousy tonight. Fucked up royally."

Bluebird sat down. The two looked at each other. The bedroom was dark. From somewhere outside, near the pool, came a high shriek, followed by group laughter.

Bluebird smiled.

Finally Cora did, too. "Authentic, huh?" she said. "History etched in skin." She walked to the closet door mirror, studied herself. Behind her she could see Bluebird sitting on the bed, head bowed, short hair pinned in a semblance of an old-fashioned knot, wisps falling against the slender neck. "Bluebird."

"Yeah."

"Haven't they told you you're beautiful?"

"Them?" Bluebird grunted. "They find it difficult to say 'Hi' to me."

"That's because you don't make it easy. You keep your distance."

"I don't hear anybody saying 'come here.'"

"I heard Debby tell you you're beautiful."

Bluebird shrugged. "And then she invited everybody but me to join her at the pool."

"She meant you, too."

"No." Bluebird stood up, unpinned her hair, and began undressing. "She meant for me not to come, and precisely because she had said I was beautiful."

Cora waited a moment, looking at them both in the mirror. The frame of Bluebird's body was lovely, wide, supple, strong; Cora's frame would fit inside. "Maybe," Cora said. "But they said you have bones that a photographer dreams of."

"You're making it up."

"What they really said is that your bone structure would give a photographer wet dreams."

"God. Really?" Bluebird was turning in quick circles, ending suddenly in a curtsy. "Really? When I wasn't even there, they said that?" High small voice.

Cora had to look away. "Really," she said.

"Why did I do it?" Bluebird threw herself against the bed, rolled over on her back. Why did I do it?"

"Because you could do it better than they could."

Bluebird sat up. "Is that why?"

Cora nodded. "And they know it, too."

"So now they'll never like me."

"Maybe."

"Because I'm better than they are."

"Maybe."

Cora had never seen anything like it. By the pool, the moonlight glistening on water, dead still air, heat, with music coming from one of the rooms, the short actress Debby had begun dancing, dressed only in her bathing suit, her movements awkward, but her eyes downcast and her hands graceful. Then Betty had joined her, then one or two of the others. Cora had been a little embarrassed, had suspected that she could do better than they, and had been tempted to try. But the picture of the group, half naked, undulating in the moonlight, held her back.

Then Cora heard a gasp, and turned as they had turned. There, on the other side of the pool, in the center of the grass lawn, was Bluebird, nude, white body sweeping softly, arms reaching up, waving out, around, up, down.

Jesus, someone said.

Bluebird had continued, alone, till gradually the others had gone in and only Cora remained. Then Cora, too, had walked to her room, aware that the dancing had stopped, that Bluebird stood there silent and naked.

Now Cora went in to the bathroom to change from her suit, slipped on panties and bra for bed.

"They asked if you studied dance," she said toward the doorway.

"And? What else?"

"I told them no. With you it's all natural."

"God. Why did I do it?"

Cora pulled back the covers. "I told you." She got in bed, lay on her side, pulled the covers over her shoulders in spite of the heat.

"Cora?"

"Yes."

"Are you jealous of me?" Bluebird was sitting on her bed, her knees drawn up, her words muffled against her skin.

"Yes," Cora said. "I wish I weren't, but I am." She turned over.

Bluebird lay, eyes open, watching the shape of Cora in bed. Bluebird thought herself tiny, curved for sleep. She thought herself timid, lined, aging. "It's because you need an audience," she murmured toward Cora's back. "They're what you draw from." She felt herself cracking into pieces and turned over, too, stared at the wall.

Bluebird showered, and Cora waited. Cora could hear the high trills, la-la-las of Bluebird's happiness, muted by the running water. When Bluebird came into the living room, she was rosy and smiling. She sat in the center of the floor, the sunlight yellow through the curtains. She took deep breaths, stretching slowly, languidly, first toward one side, then the other, then forward. At the deep part of each stretch, she groaned, long, letting the air whoosh after the voice had stopped.

"Bluebird?" Cora said.

Bluebird didn't answer.

Cora sat on the sofa, lighted a cigarette.

"Don't smoke when I'm working out. This is my room, too." Bluebird threw back her head, yelled a high "yeow," and pushed herself up quickly. "Okay. What is it?"

"They say they can hear you crying in here. Every morning when I go for coffee."

"Do they?" Bluebird lighted a cigarette, too. "Who's 'they'?"

"They say it's real sobbing, Bluebird. They thought I would know about it."

"Which you don't, right?"

Cora shrugged. "I don't know."

"Don't worry about it." Bluebird walked to the window, looked out toward the pool. "I could go out there and sit at a table, and no one would join me."

"You could join them."

"Would they talk to me?"

"If you'd talk to them."

"About what?"

"I don't know, Bluebird. Anything. Just anything."

"Okay. We'll see how right Cora Leban is about the world." Bluebird swung out the door, closed it behind her, immediately opened it again. She strode to the table, picked up her sketch pad, slipped on sunglasses, ran her fingers through her hair, fanning it wild around her face. Then she strode to the door again, took a deep breath, bowed to Cora, and opened the door. "Artist," she said, and closed the door again.

"I'm walking to the theatre tonight," Bluebird said, the minute they reached their room.

Cora tossed her purse to the sofa. "At the moment, that is

absolutely fine with me. Sulk away."

"You cut me off every time I tried to talk."

"I didn't, for God's sake, hear you."

"You weren't listening. You don't listen. And you bump into me when you're walking, just like I wasn't even there."

"Then tell me to shut up. Tell me to back off. Tell me to keep my own space."

"I'm not responsible for you, Cora Leban." Bluebird threw her purse to the sofa, too, stomped her foot, then suddenly dropped into a squat, elbows on knees, face hidden between her hands, sobbing. "You suck power, Cora. You try to suck me away into nothing."

Cora stood still. Bluebird could be five years old, younger, but the thighs, bent, were firm and full, the arms held tightly against them were curved, smooth, ending in strong hands splayed across her face like bars. Cora bent down, touched Bluebird's head with her fingertips. "That's the way people talk, Bluebird. Everybody talks that way, joins in."

Bluebird sniffed, rubbed the back of her hands into her eyes, glanced up at Cora. Her voice came out high and whiny, "'That's the way people talk, Bluebird. Everybody talks that way.'" She lay back. "You are such a wimp, Cora. Such a fucking wimp."

Cora folded her arms against her stomach, felt the thinness of her ribs. "I don't want to room together anymore," she said, looking toward the window. "I'm getting out of here."

"Of course you are. Run, Cora."

"I mean it."

"Sure. Why feel bad, Cora? Why think about yourself, Cora? Everybody knows Cora Leban is a strong woman, a strong woman, certainly not a worm." Bluebird lengthened her body, rolled to her side, stretched, rolled, smiled, stretched, "Not a worm, worm, worm."

Cora sidestepped Bluebird toward the bedroom, took her suitcase from the closet, began taking her things from the dresser.

Bluebird stood in the doorway. Then she sat on the other bed. "I'm sorry," she said.

In the bathroom, Cora filled her nightcase with shampoo, soap, toothpaste, haircombs, her eyes watching the doorway reflection in the mirror. Bluebird stepped into it.

"I was hurt," Bluebird said, her lips trembling. "I wanted you to hurt, too."

Cora just shook her head, waiting for Bluebird to move aside.

"You're the most beautiful person I've ever known," Bluebird said.

Cora held the nightcase above the bed, finally lowered it, sat down.

"I want you to like me anyhow, Cora." Bluebird watched Cora's eyes, pale blue, clear, looking everywhere but at Bluebird. She saw the lines at the corners of the eyes and mouth, the etched creases across the wide forehead. She wanted to rub them away, to moisten her fingertips and shadow the lines away, smooth them beneath the surface. "I like you anyhow."

Cora put her hands in her lap. "I can't," she said. "I'm scared of you."

Cora was going to blow the jig, she knew it. Through the gauze she could see the blur of the women's dresses as they whirled to the jig, could hear fragments of their laughter. Beside her, in the periphery of her vision, was Bluebird, but Cora would not look that way, though she knew, felt, that Bluebird was looking at her, perhaps just facing her, with eyes closed, waiting for the fiddle to reach the end of the measure. She could see the dark hem of Bluebird's dress, the high arch of one buttoned shoe.

The mandolin cut in, sharp, crisp, clear bursting prisms of sound. Cora bowed her head, listened.

How could such music come from Bluebird.

Then came the quiet; the lights lowered. At Cora's left was a soft rustle, then a tapping, light, giving the count, slower, slower. Cora raised her eyes, but Bluebird was facing the curtain, her body still; the tapping had ceased. Slow. Cora began the jig, heard it more than played it, gently, mournfully, the notes overlapping like black lace.

See? she heard from her left.

Cora lay awake all night, or so it seemed, her room quiet and dark. Once she stood and walked to the window, looking across the lawn to Bluebird's room where the light was on and where she saw Bluebird's shadow against the drapes. In the morning, earlier than she usually rose, Cora went to the cafeteria for coffee, carried it to the poolside, the air moist and cool from the water. Bluebird was there, at a round, white table, sketch pad closed before her. Cora started toward the other side, then turned back, and sat across from Bluebird, not speaking, lighting a cigarette and pushing the pack to the center of the table.

"I don't know how to help you," she said.

"I know. That's okay."

The sun lifted higher, warmed the water. Others came out waving, stumbling, smiling, toward the cafeteria. The sun became too warm. Cora and Bluebird stayed where they were. People slipped into the pool, shimmered water, gradually moved to Cora and Bluebird. Someone lifted the sketch pad. A light breeze whispered through, and Bluebird watched it catch the red silk of Cora's hair. Cora's eyes followed the line of Bluebird's hands and forearms against the table.

Cora? someone said. Why, these are of Cora, aren't they?

Are you sure? No. Wait a minute. They're Bluebird.

Cora and Bluebird looked at each other over the sketches, watched them being passed around, lined up, spread finally in a long line against the gray cement.

The Vernacular

At two o'clock on an impossibly hot Friday afternoon, Cora wished for a sense of humor, no more than that. Just a good, solid, disgusting sense of humor that would let her slap her thigh as if it were round and full, and maybe spit in an arch which she had never learned to do, and was embarrassed whenever anyone—like Tinaree's mother down the street—did.

At the moment, books abandoned, Cora was in the swelter of a University Boulevard, no-shade-trees afternoon, sitting in an abandoned building just off an alley that disguised itself as David Street. She was paint-spattered, sweaty, weary, forty-plus years, and was holding her right arm down a hole under a half-fallen door, in order to dangle a piece of raw chicken before a cat who obviously did not want to come out, not until Cora got rid of her dog, or until the cat's owner returned to send a coaxing voice down the dark recess. All Cora could muster was a guttural "God damn you blasted, shitfaced feline," and then sit rubbing the circulation back into her arm.

She had three books, at least, to read this weekend or her schedule was shot to hell.

None of her friends would use such language.

Halfway down David Street, Cora tossed the chicken into a neighbor's already fly-swarmed trashcan. Her ex-husband had been named—was named—David.

Almost at her own gateway, Cora returned to the trashcan, conceding that, fool that she was, she would try again, and might even go so far as to waste another piece of chicken if she didn't retrieve the first. She wondered, too, how many neighbors watched her, "that red-haired white woman," traipsing up and down the alley-street the past two days, various tidbits dangling from her hand.

The cat, Caliban, was her daughter's.

Her daughter was in the mountains with a man old enough

to be her father.

"For God's sake, Mother," that daughter had said, "don't tell me about your sex life."

Cora had been talking about a non-sex life, really.

Down the street, Tinaree's mother began leading her brood of illegitimates up the walk, her torso billowing as she walked as if buoyed by waves, a black balloon. She was the fattest mobile person Cora had ever seen. She was, the visiting old black man had said, a prostitute.

Cora considered again that very likely she, Cora, was prejudiced. Her mother was. And her brother. They used the vernacular, too. Without vulgarities, though.

Only Cora, among all the people she worked and played with, lived west of Main, and without tongue-in-cheek pleasure. Only Cora had to put her trashcan in front of the house for the city pickup, and stand broom-prepared for her neighbors' dogs. Only Cora would be standing with raw chicken in her hand, barefoot, white paint like a mottling disease over both legs, when Jeb drove up, antique truck running smoothly, its improvised horn ballyhooing, and Jeb swinging out broad-shouldered and young, clean, healthy, from twenty miles outside town, with an actual flowing river just a mile away.

"Got time to pick a few tunes?"

"Sure."

"Not studying today?"

"Painting." She held up the chicken, "and cat-calling."

"Want some help? I got an hour or so."

"No. Let's play."

While he was getting his guitar, Cora bent to call under the house. "Damn you for chasing that cat. You hear?" She heard the wagging tail thump against the ground. Cora had been burglarized twice and no one had heard her dog barking. "I could give you away," she whispered, but the tail thumped again. She followed Jeb into the house.

Jeb was the cleanest person Cora knew. He owed no money. He owned absolutely nothing. He could make the most beautiful, compelling knives. One of them, the last, of which Cora had taken a photograph, sold for over a thousand dollars. Cora wondered if the making of knives were phallic, and the purchasing of them, and the photographing of them.

That could be, since a photograph was a memory, and now so was a phallus. To Cora, at least. At least for a long time.

While she showered, Cora listened to Jeb playing. He was better than she, but he never acknowledged that. She supposed that since he didn't find her femininely, sexually appealing, his gift to her was finding her musically appealing. He delighted in her music, he intimated, with smiles, with requests, with nods of his head.

Cora liked his liking her very much, and that when he was tired he took naps at her house, then hugged her goodby to find a country-western band, and to dance with every single woman in the place. He had told Cora once that he always tried to dance with every single woman. Was that a gift, Cora wondered, a charity? That Cora didn't want—charity—but she wasn't sure how to distinguish appreciation from pity. When he asked Cora to come dancing, she always said no.

So this Friday afternoon, while Jeb took his nap, Cora peeled flecks of paint from her feet, resting her chin on her knees and letting her hair fall in a veil over either side of her legs. She needed a sense of humor with Jeb, too, since he was now enamored with Demares, who, until the year before, had been Elizabeth. Until the year before that one, she had been more lined than Cora, and three years before that, had been not only lined but flatchested.

Now she was buxom, and her face said no more than thirty.

Cora believed that women who had their faces lifted, much less their breasts and buttocks, were betrayers of the female sex, by their action conceding that only beauty—and a certain kind at that—equated appeal.

But on the other hand, maybe Cora's belief was just a black-mirrored jealousy, because, even if Cora did have a facelift, Demares would still be the more lovely. So maybe being against it allowed Cora to be superior in the long run.

Like not taking the exam, and therefore not failing.

Like speaking Missouri-speak so no one would ask too difficult a question.

Perhaps Cora was a fraud. People with class didn't sit and peel paint from their toes while young men slept alone in their beds.

When Demares drove up, Cora wasn't at all surprised, but she was a little angry. The last three Fridays this had happened, and while Cora liked Demares, she liked equally well Demares' husband, Walter, who was a little homely, much older than Demares, but peaceful. He fixed cars, guitars, faucets, anything broken. He smiled often. He showed Cora how to hook up her cooler in summer and her heater in winter. Cora typed letters for him, just brief notes to cousins, nephews—he believed in family, he once said—and edited them discreetly which neither he nor she ever acknowledged.

"Jeb sleeping?" were Demares' first words.

"Obviously."

"God, it's hot." Demares was at the refrigerator, pulling out a beer.

"The beer," Cora called from the sofa, "is Craig's. He said for me to save it. He may stop by after work."

"Juice, then. Better anyway. Want some?"

"No," Cora said. Demares was dressed in black leotards—her meditation outfit—blonde hair pulled up and curling wildly down, breasts full but high, perfectly symmetrical and lovely above a flat abdomen. She played harp for a group who made and sold relaxation tapes. She read books on visualization, reincarnation, self-realization, codependent behavior, and believed fidelity, on her part, to be a sign of an addictive relationship.

Demares wanted to have an affair with Jeb.

Walter, Demares' husband, during a marital hiatus, during which Demares had thrown a skillet through his car window, had let himself be seduced by Bluebird Willey.

"How long's Jeb been sleeping?"

"He asked me last week if I called you when he stopped by. Seemed pretty coincidental, he said."

"What'd you tell him?"

Even when Demares drank orange juice, she looked beautiful. She tilted her head down, the glass up, and the angle was so perfect it couldn't have been studied.

Cora picked up her coffee cup. "That I wouldn't do such a thing. Went out in my grade school days."

"Did you tell him I wouldn't do such a thing, either?"

"No."

"You're mad at me."

"Maybe."

"Over Jeb?"

"Probably. I can't get it straight."

"Need to talk about it?"

"Not now."

"Okay. But don't let it get between us."

That was why Cora liked Demares. She could find the center of things quickly, and meet it with absolutely no tremor, and someone who could do so wouldn't have a face lift for the wrong reason.

So somewhere Cora was looking at things wrong. Surely there was humor in that.

"The Greek goddess," Jeb said at his first step into the living room. Then "thanks for letting me nap," to Cora. Then to Demares, "So, lady, want to go dancing tonight?"

"Hasn't Cora worked wonders with this place?"

"Changing the subject? Yes, she has. Want to go dancing?"

He twirled in a graceful circle, empty arms holding an invisible woman. He was, Cora knew, a good dancer.

"I don't know if it would be kosher."

"We don't have to screw."

Cora liked Jeb. A lot. Just as she liked Walter, and Craig, and Milosh, who seldom came around now that he was "in love, baby, absolutely gone, found THE woman." Obviously she liked men better than women. Now was that prejudice? No. Worse.

"What do you think, Cora?" One of them had asked the question, and both of them were looking at her.

"About?" she said.

"Our going dancing together," from Demares.

"I think if you're going to do it, do it and be done with it. That's what I think." Cora slapped her hands against her knees and stood, putting her hands on her hips as she had seen too many women, even her mother, especially her mother, do. She dropped them.

"I want to finish the molding, not watch a mating ritual," she said, and was already embarrassed at her tone and what the statement, plus the tone, could not help but signify. At least to sensitive people such as these. "Sorry," she said. "Getting older isn't easy." To avoid saying "is it?" to Demares, Cora dumped out the perfectly good remaining coffee and filled the pot with tap water, and then walked out her back door. She heard the louder thumping that meant the dog was belly-crawling out to be petted, so she waited. The dog was afraid of anything that moved suddenly or sounded harsh, and the burglars had used a crowbar. Cora didn't expect any animal to be braver than she could be.

When she reentered the living room, Jeb and Demares were side by side on the sofa, and Demares was laughing, charmingly.

Cora couldn't think of a way to reenter the conversation, but it didn't seem to matter anyway.

Demares had been reading the Seth books. Had Jeb ever read them? No?

He didn't read much.

Well, Demares did, with a chuckle that made the quick thrusting movement of her breasts almost natural. She read all the time, didn't she, Cora?

Yes. And admittedly, Demares was bright. She did read all the time. She also wrote poetry, powerful, moving, twisted visions. So why, then, did Cora at this moment wish that one of Demares' breasts would explode, or come unseamed, or droop suddenly—whatever malfunctioning beauty did?

Of course, Demares was adding, she didn't read the same things Cora did. She wished Cora would read more metaphysical writers, then they could talk about them. Cora said they drove her insane. Right, Cora?

Yes. Balmy. Over the brink.

Jeb didn't believe in talking much when he was with beautiful ladies. It was a waste of art.

"Oooh," said Demares, "that's honesty for you, and a good line, too. The only flaw is 'ladies' instead of 'a lady.' Gave yourself away there."

"Except that there are two of us in the room, you know," Cora said, and almost, just almost, did feel like smiling at the expression on Demares' face.

When they left, in separate cars, but for the same place, Cora sat on her front porch. Once a man, a black man, old and stumbling up the middle of University Boulevard, had seemed suddenly to become aware of Cora on her front porch, playing her guitar. He had cupped one hand behind his ear, grinned, waved, then cupped his ear again and walked to the gate as if he were being pulled. Cora had stopped playing.

He had asked if he could come sit on her porch awhile. Back home, Cora remembered, you didn't refuse shade or water. She gave him a soda.

Remembering that, the hour he had sat, smelling faintly of alcohol, talking of women who lived alone, and how they must handle that loneliness, Cora almost went inside. He had ruined her front porch, with a fairly foul memory. She had wanted to say "get out of here"; she had wanted to say "No, you can't sit on my porch." Only when his visions of women's answer to loneliness had become graphic, had she asked him to leave. And even then she wasn't sure if she had asked him to go because he was black. After all, Walter had been graphic, though guilty, about the affair with Bluebird, and Cora had not asked him to leave. But then she and Walter were friends. Bluebird Willey and Demares were no longer friends.

Cora propped her feet on the bench in front of her, hugged her forearms against her. Maybe when she sold the house, moved, she would lighten up. Maybe it was always this way with single women.

Craig was very, very glad Cora had saved his beer. He wished she would give in and get a realtor, though.

She hated realtors.

Craig had long, brown, hiker's legs. Cora thought now, as in the past, that running her hands over the arch of his thighs would feel good against her palms. She remembered a line from a story, about such a feeling being etched into the hands. Craig took Cora to movies from time to time, trimmed her hedge, made sure she never missed a concert, even if he only called and told her where and when. Craig was now, as he put it, "interested" in Bluebird Willey. The old man had said "hot" and "want to jump her bones" about Tinaree's mother.

Bluebird Willey had been abused as a child. But Cora wasn't supposed to tell anyone. And hadn't.

Craig had herpes. And Cora wasn't supposed to tell anyone that either. And hadn't.

A year before, Cora had hinted that she and Craig go to bed together. He had, after all, been over to her house at least three nights a week, talking, laughing, drinking coffee, praising her cooking.

He was complimented. Really. But, well, he was looking for a mate, a companion, not a, a casual affair.

Then, watching television one night, after beer and pot that someone, probably Demares, had left at Cora's, he had said.

"I got herpes."

"I'm sorry."

"She was a bitch, pardon the expression. A real bitch."

Cora didn't want to know who "she" was.

"She didn't warn me at all. Debby. For months I kept getting this breakout, you know, on my chin. Here. And she never said a word."

"I didn't know," he had added, shaking his head, "that you

could get it so bad. It's on my tongue, too. My face, my tongue, and my, well, here."

So he was rarely free of it.

"It's cyclical," he had said.

Craig liked sitting on Cora's porch like this, resting, watching the sun go down. It was a genuine neighborhood, people walking the streets, sitting on the curb, in yards.

Cora had thought about buying a pistol.

Did she know how to use one?

"You just pull the trigger," she said.

He could show her how, he said, and kissed her cheek which meant he was preparing to leave, and which meant she would in a moment scour her cheek with cleanser. He patted the top of her head. He'd show her how to load it, and all.

When the sun set, Cora turned on the porchlight, and locked all the doors. The neighborhood had no streetlights, and even with no trees, when dark settled in it was complete, with just little spots of light through thin drapes or open blinds, but Cora couldn't trust who was behind there. She had tried talking to the neighbors, but she didn't know who they were. They didn't talk about Gould, or intertextuality. They said things like

"Hey, lady."

"How's it going?"

"You got a phone?"

"That your dog?"

One woman, asking if Cora had a washer, had appeared on the front porch to "visit" while she did three loads of wash. Cora had not known how to say no. After two and half hours of talk that never got past the house the woman planned to have, the job she planned to get, Cora had said no that they could not work out a deal with the washer and phone.

That woman was Tinaree's mother. Tinaree lay down in the center of University Boulevard whenever she didn't get her way. Her hair was braided like spikes.

Cora turned on the lamp by the sofa, turned the shade so the chipped place was in back, and took one of the books from the coffee table. If she could read three books a day for the rest of the summer, maybe she could pass the test. Her mother had gone through only the eighth grade; her father the sixth. Her sister was now fighting a husband for the right to nightschool. They all three believed homosexuals and blacks should be shipped out of the country, and that child abusers should be castrated at least, and probably executed.

Bluebird's father had been a preacher.

If Craig gave Bluebird herpes, was it Cora's fault?

Walter's car pulled in front of the house, and Cora hurried to unlock the screen door. She watched him carefully shut and lock the car door, and come smiling toward the house. He walked shyly, just as he talked. Cora wondered why he loved Demares, who used to be Elizabeth, who used not to be so lovely, but that was before he had met her; and Demares said what he didn't know could not at all affect their relationship, and should not, if Cora understood what she meant. Cora understood.

"Studying?"

"Yes, but come on in."

"Sure?"

"Sure. Want coffee?"

"No. I see the books. I'll come back tomorrow."

"You guys fighting?"

He shrugged, smiled a little.

"I painted the entire back room today," Cora said.

"Let me see."

He had met Bluebird Willey at Cora's house, for which Demares still had not forgiven Cora, and, in a way, neither had Bluebird, since Walter went back to Demares anyway, and now Bluebird's social circle had decreased.

"Looks good. You're still asking too much, though."

"I bought it for that."

He nodded. "You got taken."

"Why didn't you warn me it was a bad deal?"

"Should have. Demares and Debby are friends. One of them

would have killed me."

He liked his coffee with two and one-half teaspoons of sugar and almost white with canned milk. He came by often enough that the milk didn't ever go bad, even if Caliban the cat weren't visiting.

"She's mad," he said finally, "because when we ate at the Lodge in the Desert, I took a rose from the vase and stuck it in the butter."

"You know better than that."

"Yes." He grinned, and Cora liked the way he did so. He had soft chocolate-colored eyes, and bushy brows, with white beginning to show at the edges. "I thought," he said, "she might be here."

"No."

"Want to go for a hamburger?"

"No."

"Okay." He finished his coffee, stood, glanced back at Cora as he stepped toward the door. "Maybe I'll call Bluebird."

"Don't." Cora rubbed her cheek. "I'm going to put the sign up tomorrow. Maybe it'll sell fast."

"I was kidding about Bluebird. Sure you don't want to go?"

"Sure. Gotta study."

He walked to the porch, leaned back to the screen one minute. "Don't tell her I said that, okay?"

"Okay."

Cora locked the front door, left the living room light on so no one could see through the thin blinds, and took her book to bed. One side of her bed was covered with books, and she lay for a moment beside them, reading the titles, then reading the names sewn into the quilt on which the books lay: Myrtle McCray, Shelby Weaver, Marie Phillips, Virginia Leban. Fifty names if she would read them all. Two hundred books if she did the same. She had counted them. The smell of paint was heavy and she got up to shut the bedroom door, then took a few minutes to wash her face again, and rub alcohol into her cheek.

She lay down, followed the small print, noting that her

thumb nail had a blotch of paint where the moon should be. The material seemed familiar. Who was she reading? Sassure? Barthes? The lamp light wasn't bright enough; she had to hold the book too close, and it hurt her eyes. Demares wore glasses to read, but not in front of anyone. Demares was not a very good dancer. Maybe when, and if, she and Jeb lay down together, Demares would forget and lie on her back, and Jeb, slipping his hand around the curvature of her breasts, would feel the ridges, hard as the ironwood of his knives, and he would know the truth. Maybe Bluebird, crying again one morning, would see the red blemishes spread inside her thighs and know the truth.

Cora slammed the book shut, tossed it aside and stood. Only a fool would buy this house.

She turned on the light in the back room, opened the paint and began painting the molding along the floor. Maybe, just maybe, Jeb and Demares would find each other the flowing spirit they needed, and they would dance forever into reincarnated blissfulness. Maybe Craig and Bluebird would come next Friday to visit hand in hand, to announce their commitment to a joint life and companionship and unmolested children.

But then, what about Walter? Where could she put him?

Somewhere outside, a cat meowed, and the dog thump-thumped rapidly, and one of them scrambled over the aluminum side fence and one of them plowed into it. Cora took the flashlight from the linen closet, the wrapped chicken from the refrigerator, and walked purposefully, eyes and ears alert, toward the alley, wondering who had hit the street sign, so that it now turned in the opposite direction. The dark covered her path except for the narrow beam she cast before her. She eased through the trash, sat down beneath the fallen door, and turned the light momentarily down the hole. Her daughter loved this cat.

"You down there?" she said. Yes. Bright points of eyes far beneath. Cora held the chicken a few inches into the hole.

"Come on up," she said.

For a moment, it seemed the cat moved forward, then the lights of the eyes blurred backward and away.

"Have it your way." She turned out the flashlight and sat, looking at the sky, so much of it from here, the lights there, too, blurring away and into each other. Surely, from that vantage, this would look absurd, ludicrous, sitting in the dark in this neighborhood. She turned toward the rustling sounds behind and beneath her. And perhaps from down there, too. She laid the chicken at the edge of the hole, then moved to the other side of the fallen door, crossing her legs and resting her elbows against her knees. No one would know she was here, and no one could find her if he did. If she put Walter with herself, did that mean she had to have a facelift? She thought about it awhile. Then she sat, waiting on the cat, and practicing, quietly and poorly at first, spitting in an arch into the black, rubble-strewn yard.

The Sound Man

The entire music community was fond of Milosh. Every Saturday morning they woke to his deep mellow voice which sounded—as Cora had once said—like male honeysuckle if flowers could speak. They liked his chuckles over the wires, his croons to them. "Hey, baby, you think you heard bluegrass? You think you heard harmony? Coming to you now, from the hands and through the taste of Milosh Lukovich is. . . ."

The musicians and their followers would nod their heads at the radio, say "some guy" or "he's hot today" or "if he could play like he can talk. . . ."

That was, they agreed from time to time, the blight in Milosh's otherwise fairly enviable life. The guy wanted so much, so damned much, to play well. To their regret, he often thought he could. But he fiddled like a poor beginner or a senile oldtimer. His massive body, somewhat pearshaped and soft, would tense, his shoulders would curve around the fiddle, his arm would raise, his wrist having that slight arch of someone classically trained, the bow would look as if it were gliding effortlessly over the strings—but the sound, the sound.

Sometimes when this happened at various jam sessions or parties, the other musicians would continue playing with him anyhow. After all, he was a good old boy, really—he gave more parties than most, usually bought the majority of the beer, and never, never, took offense. When they didn't feel like putting solid rhythm behind his passionate fiddle howls, they simply acted as if they must leave the circle a moment, to get another beer, to go to the john, or to have a cigarette.

So when the music community, at Milosh's instigation, managed to scrape and beg enough money to bring the new band Devil Grass to their town, for a one-night, three-hour, unbelievable concert, they decided to let Milosh have the customary honor of housing the guests. That would be a reward for his constant volunteer broadcasting, for the encyclopedic knowledge he had amassed in order to fill the air not only with music, but with the heritage of music.

"Here ladies and gentlemen, friends and foes, aficionados of what's good no matter its age, is the first tune recorded by Webb Wilson. The year? 1931. The town? St. Louis. The song? You name it, friends, and you get a free t-shirt from your community radio station, KJIX."

They could just see him, dropping the needle, cuing the tape, his big body hanging over the sides of the chair in front of the turntable, his black hair mussed from his constant moving, and one dark, thick lock falling over his forehead.

"Want to know how American the banjo is? Came from Africa, fifth string added in the Appalachian Mountains so the banjo could match the drone of the fiddle, a drone that was intended to unleash into those hillbilly mountains the wailing woe of bagpipe. And here, proving that potpourri can be pure pleasure, is Earl Scruggs, plucking those intercultural strings."

Yes, the community agreed, passing the word through the upper levels of the musical hierarchy—who better than Milosh to entertain and escort Devil Grass.

The week before the concert, the Saturday morning bluegrass show featured Devil Grass every fourth song, and the subdued quality of the voice announcing the discs didn't fool anyone. Milosh was wanting to announce that he, Milosh Lukovich, would be the man of the hour, that he would be giving an after-concert party for the hottest pickers this town had ever drawn. Of course, he couldn't announce that. The rules said that only a few could be invited to the party, only the elite; the rules also said that no one should have hurt feelings. Milosh, especially on the air, had to remember the rules.

"Better bribe, borrow or steal your way to this concert, folks. You gotta see in action what cold vinyl cannot contain. But if you miss it? Not to worry. Saturday next the fine driving bow of Devil Grass's fiddler will be featured right here, the concert will be recorded and repeated, for you, and you, and you."

They could see him, rolling his dark eyes, chewing his nails to the stub. But he wouldn't, they were sure, say a word.

In the early part of the week, from his accountant's desk, where he plodded with figures and often made mistakes, Milosh called Tim Creighton, to say that he wanted to invite Cora, since the party was at his own house.

"Probably shouldn't," Tim responded, and then passed the news on to Bob Carley, his bassman. "He's asking Cora. Next it'll be Jeb Stoner, and Willard, and the whole gang."

They were right. Milosh wanted to invite everyone. "No," someone told him. "You think Devil Grass will want to jam with your regular crowd?"

Some thought the party should be open anyway.

Some thought they had made a mistake to give any part of this to Milosh.

Cora told the ladies in her band that she wasn't going to that party, and she hoped they weren't either. They were in Cora's house at the time, and had set their instruments aside for awhile, in order to talk, to retune, to wonder if they were poor musicians. The blonde, stocky one, whose voice always turned heads, who made older women smile and younger men think "if she would lose some weight," said "If I went, someone would just borrow my mandolin. I'd never get to play."

The darkhaired one, older, whose autoharp found bluegrass and blues as well as ballads, said "I couldn't sing in front of that crowd, anyway."

"They just want us to listen," Cora said. She was the oldest, and the smallest, and the one who worried the most that maybe they weren't good.

By Wednesday, the entire group knew that Milosh was host for Devil Grass, that he had half-emptied his previously crowded living room so "Devil Grass could practice." He had ordered "two hams. Hams? They're pigs. Gigantic. I could feed history. Feed the world."

He had his fiddle "set up" by Pop Bradshaw.

He was getting up at five to practice before he went to work.

"He's dug up some tune he says they'll kiss him to learn."

"Cora says he really does have a good tune. Some old-country thing. Maybe Devil Grass is what the guy needed. Got him in gear."

"Maybe. But what does Cora know about fiddling?"

"Yeah. What's she play anyhow?"

"Guitar. She backs him up sometimes."

"Oh yeah. That's right."

Devil Grass slept all of Friday morning. They slept in beds with new sheets stretched tighter than nerves, with an electric fan running in each room just to soften sounds, so Milosh could work without disturbing them. When they straggled awake one at a time he met them with offers of juice, eggs, ham, coffee, lunch.

They had never had it like this, they agreed.

One said, "the guy gave me his card. Look." The card was gray, with black print.

Milosh Lukovich
man of sound
mind, body and music

They laughed, tossed the card on the coffeetable.

Then they practiced. They played beginnings over and over, eyes meeting, cuing now, start, again, one and a two and a. They were not once interrupted, though this thick shadow occasionally moved from the sofa to the chair, from the chair to the sofa arm, and three or four times sat quietly holding a fiddle.

"Beer? Coffee?" they heard during pauses.

"Thanks. We never been treated like this."

"Nice place you got here."

"Hear you push our album."

When they finished in the late afternoon, the back yard was cool, shaded by giant elms, and they found him out there, sitting alone, fiddling, which he continued for a moment after they had all joined him, and then put the fiddle down as if he were puzzled. "Not an easy tune," he said. "You guys wanta eat something now?"

"No, we'll wait'll after the concert. What was that you were playing?"

He said something they couldn't understand, smiled, said "Serbian tune. *Fool's Dance.*"

"Nice tune. Play it again."

Finally, they went for their instruments, had him play it again and again.

Catchy tune, they agreed.

Not everyone went to the concert, but still all the chairs were filled, people lined the walls, filled the doorway, came filtering in late, so the ticket taker would be gone. Some roamed the halls outside the concert room, smoking, looking at pictures of people they didn't know and saw clearly. Rules were rules. If they were around after the concert, they could crash the party. If they overheard of a party, they could go. Everyone knew.

Some listened carefully but didn't applaud.

"Flash grass," came floating down the rows.

"Who said that?"

"Sounds like Cora."

On the second row were all those to whom Milosh had given tickets, and who, he said, had to come to his party, had to. They looked at him often, sitting there beaming, foot tapping, hand slapping his thigh.

Such a man, a fun-loving man.

He's the one got the concert here.

Think he'll get uppity?

Him? Never.

From the stage, songs whipped, snapped, harmony hung together like loving angels hovering above the crowd.

Milosh's yelling alone deserved their encore.

Look how happy he is.

Late that night, strings of street lights wavered above trails of cars headed for Milosh's house. "Milosh, the big guy. Isn't he having a party?"

His back yard was packed, as was his front yard and his house. Paper plates, with traces of thin sliced ham and potato salad were like large soiled flowers on his lawn. Guests accepted another beer, and another, and followed his directions to the bathroom, to the bedroom, to Devil Grass, who were playing in the premium spot, back near the garage, where the yard light formed center stage.

Hey, Milosh. Get your fiddle boy. You haven't played a bit.

Nah. They don't need me.

We're not talking about need. Get your fiddle and get out here.

Along one wall, sitting balanced atop the concrete, were Cora and her ladies, feet dangling, eyes watching the musicians playing in the dim light.

Around Devil Grass, like a spreading shadow, were other musicians, holding mute instruments, waiting, thinking about moving off to some corner where they, too, could play.

They moved aside for Milosh and passed his call toward the wall.

Cora. Hey. Milosh says get your guitar, back him up.

Her white hands raised up empty, pointed at someone in the center group.

Milosh moved through the group, smiling, his fiddle on his shoulder, already tuned.

"D minor," someone said. "He says D minor."

"Little song I know," Milosh said, cocking his head toward the Devil Grass fiddler. "D minor for *Fool's Dance*."

"Yeah. Great tune there, great tune."

The sharp, crisp tone flew over them like a cry, plaintive, mournful, unbelievably fast, fast and driving and sad, too, so everyone stopped, stopped talking, eating, drinking, and for that one moment looked only toward the music. There Milosh stood, fiddle on his shoulder, bow up but unmoving, then starting to move, as if he might play, but no, he didn't. Devil Grass had the tune. The song went on too long, and talk began again. Milosh stood smiling, nodded once, as if yeah, yeah, that's the way it should sound.

When Milosh asked for Cora, moments later, no one knew where she had gone, but they thought someone, maybe Tim, had her guitar. She wouldn't leave without her guitar, would she?

She's done it before.

No one knew what happened to the party; it just fell apart, although people were still there at dawn. They sat in small groups, strumming away, plucking away, subdued, talking. They found it odd that a guy like him, Milosh, owned his own home, didn't get married.

Someone had heard that he was scared of women, except older ones.

Not that guy.

Someone else had heard that he'd had a pretty tough dad. Cut the kid's bike up with a hacksaw.

Where'd you hear that?

Who knows? He got locked out once, too, for being late. Had to walk five miles in the snow, and he was eight years old.

Milosh?

What kind of name is that anyhow?

No one was sure.

Some were still there when Milosh carried his records and tapes to the car. He said no, that he didn't need any help, that he did this every Saturday, and that there was more ham in the kitchen if anyone was hungry. Others wended home, some heading for bed, some for the radio, some for the radio and their tape machine.

At the regular time his deep, rich voice came over the wires, "up and at 'em bluegrass fans, wake up fellow fellows and listen to the man with the sound in this bluegrass town."

They smiled.

"If you missed the concert last night, you missed a lifetime chance to sit low and ride high, and friends, friends, sweet friends of mine. . ."

They thought his voice cracked, could see him smiling at

109

someone in the studio, or having trouble lowering the needle after a night of party and play.

". . . friends, you missed it forever. Here today, gone tomorrow, or here yesterday and gone today. But for each and every one of you, to tease your ears and please your souls, I'll spin for you the sweetest notes. . . ." At first they couldn't place the group at all. Was it an old-time band?

Someone called and guessed maybe Maybelle Carter.

Tim figured it out, but he didn't call.

Someone did, though. "That's Cora's group."

"And the name? We got a caller, folks, who knows a singer, but not the name of the band. Shall I give it away? Done. Lass Grass, Lass Grass, Lass Grass. Got that?"

Then he played Pop Bradshaw, a tape "from the Cowhand Bar, made I think, six years ago. You know, Pop has played in this town thirty-five years. . . ."

"Jeb Stoner wrote this tune, folks, and writes songs like he makes knives, with passion and precision. . . ."

He never played Devil Grass at all.

Even the radios that had been turned off, were turned on again. Even people who didn't like the songs, and weren't sure right now that they liked the man who played them, sat and listened, to every song, every name, every note, and most closely to the timbre of his voice over the wires. They weren't sure why they were listening, but they knew when they heard the final song. "An old tune," his soft voice announced, "a real old tune, meant to be played with feeling."

The record must have been very old, have been played over and over. The melody rose, faded worn and lost, then rose again. It was slow, mournful, not bluegrass at all, but hauntingly familiar.

The Prowler

It was not the right time in Cora Leban's life for a flasher, or a peeper, or a planner, to come looking in her window, but of course he couldn't know that, standing under the thick vines that clustered and fell, the leaves like delicate hand fans, just outside the floor-length window of Cora's dining room. Cora's house sat a decent distance from the street and the eaves were deep, the vines quite dense, and thus she, or anyone, she reasoned, could leave drapes open without that being an enticement. After all, anyone would have to cross her lawn, and slip between two huge, well-watered oleanders before he could approach that window, and would have to stand in a plant box in order to press up closely, as he had done.

But the policeman suggested it was her fault.

"Your whole living room is visible a block away, lady. The farther back you stand, the better you can see."

"But he was at the side window."

"Guys like this, they stake a place out. Sometimes days, weeks, months. He probably knew right where you'd be."

"How could he know if I didn't even know?"

"Well, he knew."

He did not, but Cora didn't have anything else to say to either policeman. They offended her sense of justice and timing. First, they were overweight, and it was Cora's opinion that no policeman, no fireman—no whatever or whoever's job it was to rescue people from disasters or themselves or other people—should be overweight, or overrude or overcallous. So Cora stood with her slender forearms tightly folded across her thin ribcage, her blouse somewhat pointy from fear or chill or anger, and when Cora noticed one policeman staring, she released her arms and sucked in her stomach so her breasts, tiny as they were, would sag as much as they could and soften the nipples and the policeman's gaze.

Second, it had taken them twenty-five minutes to find her house, though a helicopter had, with an obscene beam, alerted the entire neighborhood that something was amiss at that Cora Leban's place—you know the one; who lives with young men and carries that guitar in and out of the house. Cora sensed the curtains being pulled back, doors opening, eyes darting toward clocks.

"Thank you for coming," Cora said.

"You best close those drapes, ma'am."

"No."

"Really. He could come back, you know, though that would be rare. He's probably scared to death."

"I'm sure he is." Cora locked the door behind them, turned her back against it, leaned, and there it was. Fear. Not of the man, but of not knowing.

She could not go to bed; certainly not. She could not close the drapes, because then he could be outside and she would not know it, which all her life had been far worse than facing anything.

"But they rarely do anything, the peepers. They just look," the one policeman had said, the less-fat one, with the moving eyes, and the thighs that were too thick for him ever to chase anyone without raising blisters on himself.

What did "rarely" mean? And if he came over just once more, wouldn't that be rare? And sufficient?

She could see her reflection in the large square panes of the window—little segments of Cora Leban. That's what she had thought she was seeing earlier, when she stood up from her chair in front of the stereo, balanced her guitar in the three-pronged stand, checked that her electronic tuner was off, raised her eyes and saw segments of Cora Leban, only larger: blue jeans, white shirt, red bandanna. Then the realization, like boom, boom, flash, flash, that is not me. And he ran before she did.

"Was he masturbating, ma'am?" That had been the big policeman, the one with a voice like two tons of gravel, and similar skin, but kind eyes. Cora liked kind eyes.

"How should I know?" she said.

"Usually he masturbates. If it's Bandanna Tom. This is his area."

"He has an area?"

"He's been working in this part of town a few years."

"How? With policemen and helicopters and. . ."

"Look, Ms. Leban, it isn't our fault, you know. You might keep your drapes shut."

Cora might have. But she wasn't going to. The peeper had simply chosen the wrong time to press close to her window.

For one thing, Cora was forty-five, though she looked in her early thirties. She had long, thick, straight hair the deep red of tamarack sap. Her eyes were large, the eyebrow ridges wide and arched, the pupils the blue of postcard skies. She was forty-five, tired, and had been divorced for five years. In the first of those five years, she had dated many men and had thought them perhaps to be better people than she gave them credit for. She didn't want to be a hardened woman. She also thought she would perhaps go, if not mad, then from neurotic to toxic phobic if she had no rules in her life. So she settled on one of the men, for two years; and then had come upon another one, for two years. The last had been gone now since February, and Cora was trying to learn to live all alone. But not alone with some man hiding in the dark.

Cora called Milosh. He was the next-to-last and wanted, so he said, that they "be friends forever. You can be godmother to my children." That he had said sometime in the last month of the relationship. Cora, who had dieted through their two years, had almost sandpapered her face, and had slept on the edge of waking so she could keep her stomach pulled flat in case Milosh's hand draped over her waist, had believed "godmother" to be a great deal like "grandmother."

"A prowler? Messing with my Cora?" Click went the phone. Milosh loved emergencies. Cora was left with the receiver in her hand, the humming silence of a disconnection, but felt strangely comforted that a voice had been on the other end and was now speeding to her house. Only, she knew Milosh—he had one speed—his. While he was slipping on his pants, he would call his father up north to tell him about it. If he had difficulty finding his socks beneath the *Playboys*, he would also call his cousin, only recently here from Yugoslavia and who needed, Milosh said, to be included in everything.

Cora continued to stand with the phone in her hand, watching her paler but darker self outside the window. Headlights through the front panes made her hang up the phone and walk quickly to the front door, where appeared, not Milosh, but the big policeman with the kind eyes.

"Miss. We really can see you from a block away."

Just then, of course, Milosh screeches into the driveway, slams the car door, runs up on the porch, pushes the policeman aside, and grabs Cora. "God. You're okay."

"He's Serbian," she said to the policeman.

"Make her close the drapes, buddy."

"Gotcha. You bet," with a Serbian thumbs-up and a jutting jaw and a big hand on Cora's backside to push her through the door.

"You touch my drapes and no godmothering."

"Come on. You heard what the man said."

"Don't touch my drapes."

Milosh reared back, which he loved to do at bar counters if someone spoke to her, or if someone hassled her while she was performing. He reared back, and proceeded to turn out all the lights.

Cora bit her lip.

When they got in bed, he stripped first, stood smiling at Cora who lay flat on her back, hands on belly.

"No lovemaking," she said.

"What?" as if they both knew she was kidding. He slipped in beside her and Cora scooted so that her right margin was beyond the bed.

"No sex. Just company."

She felt his fingertips on her thigh, his right arm burrowing beneath her pillow. He was so huge, she would roll right into him did she not hold her breath as if she were ballasting a ship.

"Okay. that's it." She threw her legs over the edge, grabbed her pillow, plopped it on the floor, and stretched out parallel with the bed.

He stared at her a moment. "You're serious."

"Yes."

Silence. Then a harumphing sound. Then a sigh. Then, "get back in bed. I'll leave you alone."

"Promise."

"Promise."

He did not understand, he told her the next morning, why she would not close the drapes. He did not understand why she would not make love with him. They had been lovers not so long ago; he cared about her, cared deeply. Remember the time, during their affair, when she had been stranded out in Fairview? It still hurt him that she had called her ex-husband, and not him. He wanted to be the one to save her.

And he couldn't eat the scrambled eggs unless she had either peppers or chilies. Did she?

"Not in a long time. Jack didn't like them."

"He was a creep. A bum. How you took up with him I don't know. Better watch where you're headed Cora. How about cheese? Got cheese?"

She was not going to add anything to the eggs; he ate them or he did not eat them. She did not even like cooking eggs.

"This for the man who saved your life?"

Milosh, one time, had been wonderful. Milosh had taken her dancing, brought her bagels in bed, cooked, watered plants. But Milosh had cooled only a little more slowly than tepid water, and a lot less smoothly.

"My family thinks I shouldn't date a woman I can't marry."

"I don't want to marry again, thank you."

"They want me to have children; continue the family name."

"I can't have any more children."

"I know. How can they do that without a scar?"

"I told you once."

"Yeah. Ugh."

"Besides, I've had my children."

"They're beautiful, too. Did you ever worry that I might be more attracted to them than to you?"

Interwoven, surely, had been sweetness, kindness. Surely. Or Cora Leban had been and was one of the most pathetic of statistically defined divorcees.

"Want me to stay tonight, too?" Milosh asked, scooping up the eggs that Cora had not eaten,, and carrying all the plants to the sink where he began to run water. He was always neater than she, too.

"No. I'll be all right. I'm going to call David."

"Don't," he said, with a down-drooping face that looked pained. "Let me stay. Please."

"No. I'm going to call David."

David was the ex-husband, a policeman, and on the rape detail, which somehow bespoke to Cora all the reasons why a madman could stand outside her window at two a.m. and pretend to be her reflection.

When he returned her call, he said "Yes?" rather than "Hello," which had been their relationship since she left him, and before, really, which is why she had gone. Cora, however, still thought him to be one of the best men she had ever known, and felt she had done him the greatest service by leaving him. After all, twice, when he had been called out on a nighttime SWAT detail, she had had fantasies of his dying, of some gunman aiming right at David Foreman, or of David's own stumbling forward, falling, discharging the bullet into himself rather than the fleer. So, although it was all right to stop cooking when she turned thirty-eight, to stop ironing, to begin sleeping in the nude, it was not all right if she fantasized her husband's death. That kind of internal monologue one listens to.

"Did you know I had a prowler here last night?"

"No."

"Well, I did. It scared me to death."

"They usually don't hurt anyone."

"Could I have the .38 anyway?"

"Aren't you overreacting a little, Cora?"

"Can I have it?"

"It's probably not a good idea."

Cora put her feet closely together and studied the frayed tips, where tiny threads showed her pink socks. If she poked her toes up one little bit, the threads would snap.

"I guess I could buy one," she said.

Silence again. But if it were to be "no," it would have already come. David loved doubt, for other people. He would hold it like a tiny pre-shower cloud in his face and in the movements of his hands and drip it through the house. But then he had a tough job, David did. Being a cop wasn't easy, he had told her, as had other officers. And he was, he always added, "Damn good at it, Cora." He had a little-boy face, and shy mannerisms, and was a little in awe of women and nudity, and was the most respected rape detective in the department. Women always felt at ease with him. Everybody always liked David. Not everybody always liked Cora. Especially Cora.

Cora hung up the phone, walked outside, examined, on her hands and knees, the flowerbeds up close to the house. There were footprints in the front bed; and footprints in the side bed; and her tennis shoes only fit the very center of those prints. She supposed policemen did not have to check if the man had once stood there, since he had already gone. She walked to the back of the house and there, by the faucet which dripped a constant, fine line to the back hedge, were more prints. Not only prints, but three concrete blocks, stacked just below her bedroom window. Cora brushed her hands against her jeans and looked at her palms for want of anything else that she could see at the moment.

"Damn," she said toward the concrete blocks, and then looked over her shoulder and toward the side of the house where more oleanders grew thick and high, with deceptively pale pink and white blossoms. Then, biting her lower lip again, and very aware of the movement of the wind chimes and the vines and the too heavy sound of her own closing of the door, she went inside. Then she locked every door and opened the closet and slid back the shower curtain with a bread knife in her hand.

Knife beside her on the carpet, Cora took up her guitar, checked the tuning, cocking her head and closing her eyes to concentrate on the merging of the fine lower tones that meant they were in pitch. Then she flicked on the tuner and checked each string. The high ones were off; considerably off.

She lay back, stared at the ceiling, rolled her head toward the side window. Well, sweet creep, are you out there? In broad daylight, you say? No way? Creep. Nighttime crawler. She sat back up and settled her guitar across her lap, retuned each string by watching the electronic needle hover above the red line. Yes, Cora, here. Four-forty, standard pitch.

She turned on the tape recorder. "Jack. Hi. Have finally learned *Cuckoo*, Taj Mahal style. Didn't think I could do it, did you?" She turned the tape off and thought of Jack saying "Stop putting yourself down, Cora. It gets old." She erased the message, began again. "Jack. Hi. Had some excitement here last night, cellophane type. A flasher, outside the window in the wee hours." Off went the tape.

Someone, Jack, considers Cora Leban worth viewing.

Sickos, Jack, are who like Cora now.

God. Cora pushed rewind.

"Jack. Hi. Here's *Cuckoo*, Taj Mahal style."

Jack had been the second long-term lover. Cora had been playing at the Unicorn afternoons, hoping they would choose her to fill the newly vacant nighttime set. But the day of the auditions, she knew better. The young man had bent over his guitar, long wiry hair making him a male Medusa. His lips worked slightly with the difficult passages, eyes unable to meet the audience in spite of the applause.

"You were wonderful," Cora had said toward his back as he put the guitar in the case. "Really good."

"Thanks. So were you."

"No I wasn't. I'm okay. Afternoon good."

When he got the evening spot, he insisted that she join him for a few songs. He held back on his playing, and she knew it.

"Don't," she said, when they were stepping from the stage, "don't you ever hold back for me. I can take care of myself." Then she walked swiftly, hair swaying, into the back room, and the women's restroom, where she flushed every commode, turned on all the spigots and said "jebe, jebe, jebe" into the mirror. It was Serbian for "fuck" and the most satisfying word she had ever learned.

Jack was the only man she had ever known to storm into a women's john. He turned off the spigots very slowly. In the mirror, his back reflection, slender shoulders, curly hair, looked much like a young girl's. "Look," he said, still not able to meet her eyes for more than a second. "I was a shit ass."

When they began living together, Cora wrote letters to her daughters. "Don't come by to visit for a while. You would lecture me about my lifestyle."

"You could get him to dress neater, Mother."

"Nobody wears their hair long anymore."

Was all they said when they met him.

Cora had read about older women and younger men. It was the rage, the fashion, the new statistics; primitive tribes, one article boasted, often left the training of young men to the older women.

Once David had dropped by, to bring a dividend check, and Cora had wanted to explain why two guitars were on the floor, why shoes and socks were by the sofa, why six beer cans glowed a metallic pyramid in the morning light, and why the house smelled like pot.

She had taken the check, said "Thank you," and had clasped her pink robe collar with her right hand. "I don't smoke it."

"Doesn't matter to me in the least what you do, Cora."

"Yet," she said to his back as she shut the door.

If she could have put the three of them together, she would have.

Cora turned the tape on one more time. "Had a prowler here last night. Will tell you more later. I'm learning *Rock Salt and Nails*. Good luck at Winfield."

He would, of course, have good luck. Young women would listen, and watch that mouth. Cora liked young women. She wished them well. The day would come when the light streaming in the bathroom window would show crepey lines at the corner of smiles. They would sleep on their backs, holding their breath. Cora always watched young women now, knew every feature of their faces, every fine tune and turn of their youth and future. She had always been honest.

For one year, Jack's eyes had lighted at the sight of her, had followed the movements of even her wrist, hands on a cup. For the next year, he had played more, often offered to help her. Cora had begun taking her guitar out back to tune and to practice. "You make too much of it," he had said.

Jack didn't know, of course, anymore than did David, or Milosh. Or the peeper, for that matter. At first, Cora had noticed this high sound, just inside her scalp above her ears, a sound like a fine wire humming, humming high enough to break, and she thought it was because Jack was going to leave. Then came tiny whirring noises, sometimes clicking, and shifts of the high whine. Then she had seen a cricket in the bathroom off and on for two days and not once had heard it chirping.

"High frequency loss," the doctor had said. "We'll have a specialist check you."

Down, down, down, she was going. Sometimes, they said, it just happens. That's when she bought the tuner.

So, when Jack had said in February that he might leave in June, Cora had said "Why not now?" Fantasizing June from February was like fantasizing death in midmarriage.

Milosh had liked her being alone again. Her girls came to commiserate with her; they knew how hard it was to break up relationships. Cora told them if they ever had children, she absolutely would not babysit, but the girls kissed her goodbye anyway.

She wasn't the least bit sorry about any of it, Cora considered, while she wrapped foil over the tape and stuck it in an envelope. Better faced and fought; she would middle-age and old-age with a straight back and deaf ears. Who cared.

"You be careful with this," David said, and handed Cora the pistol with one hand, and dropped cartridges in her open palm with the other.

"Of course. I'm always careful," Cora said. "How you doing?"

"Fine."

"How's Martha?"

"Fine," but with a turn of his head on that one. Obviously ex-wives should not ask about new wives. "I talked to Wheeler and Fields about the prowler, Cora. They said you had the drapes wide open."

"I still can't bear to feel confined."

"Better get another lover then," he said. He looked over his shoulder as he walked to the car, and Cora blew him a kiss.

"Come hear me sing," she said. "Two p. m., prime time. Like a living rerun. You like reruns."

It gained her a rigidity in his stroll to the car, and a not once looking back at her. Cora stood twisting her hair, and biting her lip again. She finally turned to her front door, and shut it behind her as if it were her own front door and she could shut it as she damned well chose.

Cora put the pistol on the dining room table and positioned the barrel toward the window. Then she loaded it, put it back, and scooted the table nearer the window.

"Now look in," she said.

At the Unicorn, the Serbian had already struck, having used his lunch hour to announce her adventure and his role.

"Milosh said you had a prowler?"

"Did he pass out flyers?" Cora asked.

"He said he plans to stay with you until they catch the guy."

She had to use the tuner on the stage, and it took too long.

Cora had no sooner ripped David's note from the door, "Close the drapes, Cora. You're being stupid," and put her guitar on the coffee table, than the phone rang.

"Jack? Just mailed you a tape."

"Milosh called this morning. Said you'd had some trouble."

Cora curled into a corner of the sofa, pulled her hair over her shoulder. "Nothing much. A flasher."

"You okay?"

"Sure."

Silence. He had been the quietest of them all. He only said something if he meant it. He had told her she had pretty feet, skin, eyes, hair.

"Some weirdo is all. David gave me a pistol."

"You know how to use it?"

"Of course."

"Sure?"

"I said so. It's loaded. Ready."

"Is Milosh with you?"

"No."

"Did he check out the house for you?"

"No."

"Why don't you do it now, while I'm on the phone. I could hang up, call the police.

"All right. fine." Cora laid the phone down, waited, studied the gray pistol shining in the lamp light. She picked up the phone again. "All clear on the frontier."

"You should let him stay."

"I did *Cuckoo* tonight, Taj Mahal. Went over well."

"Good. What else?"

"Same stuff. *Little Omah, She Caught the Katy, Desperados.*"

"Nice set."

He talked in a vacuum; the songs he had played, the guys at the bar. No females in the periphery of old lovers' conversations.

"I'm seeing someone," she said. "You might as well know."

"I'm glad."

And he was. His voice was lighter. She had forgotten how responsible the younger generation was.

Before they hung up, he told her he was seeing someone, too. "Good," Cora said.

Cora stayed on the sofa for a long time. The house seemed too still, a little chilly. She made herself walk into every room, flick on every light, open the closets. "Not here, are you?" she said. She returned to the living room, but she didn't feel like playing. She sat on the floor, stared at the back windows, the dense leaves beyond like an overhang to an entrance. She put on an album, continued watching the window. If she squinted her eyes, she could see the table reflected in the glass, wavery. She sat crosslegged, listening to the song again and again. She leaned so her hair fell forward and she plaited it into long, thick ropes. She stood and walked toward the window, holding onto the tips of each braid. "Like this?" she said.

The peeper didn't come for a long time, so long that Cora had taken to falling asleep again, even though her doors were unlocked. She would lie in the darkened room feeling that black was a more silent color than white, wondering how she would know it was not Milosh who would come slipping up the hall, or Jack, or even David for that matter. She would close her eyes and play that scene, that it was the wrong one, and too late. But what reason would any of them have to come back? Sometimes she would fall asleep before the dawn light made the curtains transparent and she could see just the pattern of the curtains shaping the glass beyond. Her head would become heavy against the pillow and finally her mouth would open a little, and she would turn onto her side in her sleep, like a baby, dark red hair against the white sheet.

When he came again, he must have thought it odd that the door was not locked, but then the woman in the house was a strange one, standing on the porch sometimes, striking at the wind chimes with her fist. The carpet was thick, and soft. The house smelled like coffee. The phone was on the dining room table.

In the bedroom, Cora's head on the pillow turned, and her eyes fluttered open. She pushed herself up, pulled up her knees, stared at the doorway. Then she pulled the pistol quietly from beneath the other pillow and waited.

He lay as she had always thought they would lie, and she wondered how she could know that. There was the problem of how to get past him to the living room and the phone, just as always. So she lay in the bed until she was aware that he was asking for help, definitely asking for help. With the pistol clutched in both hands, pointing down at him, she made him drag himself away from the doorway, and then she stepped around him and through the door. She walked down the hall sideways, afraid that he would come from the bedroom or that one would await her in the living room. But she had timed it right. She stood, pistol in hand, and stared at the phone. She did not know who to call. Finally, she laid the receiver on the table and pushed the number with her left hand, then lifted the receiver to her ear. She asked for the police station. She wanted to tell them she had shot a man, but she caught the sight of her reflection in the window, the vines brushing against the glass, dark leaves silently moving, and she said simply that she had a prowler and they might send someone.

The Family Stone

All day the window fan had hummed, stirring only a little draft through Oida's house, where her two sisters and her two daughters had spent the day visiting. The women had eaten only cold foods in order not to heat the kitchen, and they scooted the table next to the window to catch every bit of the drawn air. Then they found hearing one another difficult, and had to speak loudly to keep their voices from warbling away.

Once Dellie had tried to get a round of gospels going, but Cora and Ruth wouldn't sing, so Dellie just said "If your grandfather was alive, we'd all be singing. You should have heard him lead the songs back then. People couldn't help but join in." Dellie was the robust aunt, who even at sixty still sang as if all the parts were hers and she couldn't bear a reedy harmony if she had a spare breath at all.

"Why don't we drive out there? To Buxton cemetery?" This came from Janey, the skinny aunt, who stood in the kitchen doorway with her arms folded across her waist. "Tomorrow's Memorial Day, and we ought to do it anyway. Let's just pile in the car and go now."

Oida began stacking the pictures. "I don't think so. You go ahead. Cora and Ruth, too, if they want."

The two younger women glanced at their mother.

"Go on," Oida said. "I just want to be quiet a while. It wears me out talking so much."

"Well, girl, you know what the answer to that is." Janey had taken her group of pictures from the table and was now in the hallway, purse in hand. "You could try talking less."

Dellie put one finger to her lips as she scooted the chair back to the table. "If she wants to rest, let her rest. You girls coming? Do you good to show some respect for your grandfather."

The cemetery was cooler than either Oida's house or the car had been, but still they plucked at their blouses and skirts as

125

they walked.

"You girls are getting along better, I guess," Dellie said. Neither Cora nor Ruth responded, but Dellie ignored that. "Good. We only got each other, you know."

They stopped at a lot near the center, marked by two matching headstones, fairly small, black. Cora and Ruth stood apart watching their aunts. A wide shadow swept across the lot and Ruth looked up, then began humming. Cora took out a cigarette.

"You going to smoke here?" Janey said.

"Yes, I am." Cora lighted the cigarette, held the match. "I didn't know Granddad put a stone up for your mother."

"He didn't, hon. Dellie and me had these put up two years ago. Dad did make one for her, though."

Janey hurried to bend down and brush at the dark, flat slab. "See here? He's carved Mom's name and the date right across here. See that?"

At Oida's again, they had to stand on the porch, the sun almost gone now, night bugs swarming the yellow light.

"She hears us. She's just upset and making us wait because we went out there."

"You hush, Janey," Dellie said, and rapped on the door again. "Oida? Oida? We're back."

They heard the scrabble of the bolt, and the door opened to a dark living room, Oida standing there bent, her eyes puffy, her lips pulled down. "I just couldn't wake up. I heard you, but I just couldn't rouse." She moved away slowly, her hand gripping a chair back momentarily before she stepped around it and sank down into it. "I don't know why I get so tired. Sometimes I get so tired I'm afraid I might just die."

*   *   *

"It dead-ends, Momma. I'll have to drive across their backyard to get to the top this way."

The three sat in the sweltery car, staring at the yard that had

126

been undriven through long enough that the grass was a thick, uniform mesh. One giant tree shaded the back yard, but its shadows fell short of the car.

"They couldn't have shut it off completely." Oida leaned forward as if she could see through the trees covering the hill. Cora put the car in reverse. "We'll go around front. Maybe they changed the entry."

In the back seat, Ruth sang the first two lines of a gospel, and then stopped. In a moment, she sang them again.

Oida sighed.

The road in front of the house was narrow, the beige rocky ruts just broad enough for the tire, and centered with a row of grass beginning to brown. The road continued to the east of the house and then up the hill.

"Oh good," Oida said.

Ruth sang two lines from another song, then went back to the first.

"You sing like Momma," Cora said.

"I wish I did. You sing more like her than I do."

They were quiet the next few moments.

"Don't worry about it," Oida said. "Ruth, you go on singing if you want."

The slope was gentle at first, but the last ten yards were steep, the road seeming to disappear at the top. Cora gunned the car and Oida held onto the window frame.

Except for the graveyard itself and the narrow roadway, they were surrounded by trees, one burning color shading into the other, the ground covered by fallen branches, clumps of dead leaves, some newly fallen, others half rotten, more soil than plant. The center clearing, though, was all hot, sharp, sunlight, making the few containers of plastic flowers too vivid, garish blues and oranges and lavenders.

"Someone takes care of the place," Cora said.

"She's down this way." Oida was walking away, her hand shielding her eyes from the sun. "Dad always thought she was over there, but he waited too long to come back here. He got it wrong."

Cora and Ruth separated to walk one on either side of their mother. They were small women, slender, one with long straight red hair, the other with short dark auburn. Their mother was even smaller, not quite plump, her back hunched severely, but she, too, had red hair, curly, sprinkled now with gray. They were all dressed as if for church, in skirts and blouses, stockings.

"I remember," Oida said, "that when I ran around the people and to the road, I was on the steep part, so it couldn't have been back there." She turned to touch Cora's arm. "See?" She pointed at the road. "Right there, when the drop starts. I was standing here and I ran around the people and that's where I ended up. It couldn't have been where Dad says." She pointed again, beyond the car. "See? The road's flat there."

"And he put down a limestone?"

"Yes. But it washes away, you know? Limestone doesn't last."

"But you found it, right? Six years ago?"

"I don't know. I don't know." Oida stood still, looking back at the car, her gaze slipping past Ruth, past Cora, down the slope. "Dad says when he came back, they had buried someone else where she was, and he found a piece of the limestone down in the gully."

"Just a piece though, right?" Cora said, stepping into her mother's line of vision.

"But the rest could be anywhere," Oida said. "Could have been in the gully too, washed away. Nobody owned this land then. Was just a hill. Then they started buying plots and no telling who's down there. People can't do anything, since they can't prove anything."

Ruth slipped her arm around Oida's waist, looked at Cora. "Where is it, Momma" she said, "the grave with the limestone marker?"

Oida walked onward again. The graves were very close together. She stopped at a sunken patch. "This is it." A short distance behind her were large gray blocks, three of them, the family names on a black patch in the center. "That family probably own this lot, too," she said.

Ruth knelt, resting her hips against her heels. "This is limestone, isn't it? Look Cora." She tugged at a mat of grass, and it ripped backward. She sat down, brushed at the dirt. "The rock goes way back under here."

Cora knelt on the other side, pulled at the grass, then searched for a stick to prod down for the edge of the stone. "Goes way back," she said. "I can't find the end."

Oida was bending over between them, her shadow on the stone. "See right here? It looks like it's been broken off. That could have been the piece Dad found in the gully."

"Limestone wears away, too, doesn't it?" Cora asked. "If he had carved her name, it might have worn away by now."

"Yes," Oida said, still bent, "it wears away."

From below the hill came the sound of a motor, and Oida turned to watch the road. Cora and Ruth continued pulling back tufts of grass, cutting at the mesh of roots. Their hands and forearms were covered with dirt.

Ruth rubbed at a groove in the stone. "Does this look like an M?"

"It doesn't look carved. Just a natural groove."

"It wouldn't look carved after all these years, would it?"

"I don't know."

A white truck shot over the hill, stopped next to their car. Cora stood up, took her cigarettes from her skirt pocket and walked away from the grave, toward the gully. Ruth watched her, but continued pulling at the grass. Their mother was looking toward the truck.

"That might be the caretaker," Oida said. In a moment she walked a few feet toward the truck, then stopped. "There's two of them."

"You could ask anyhow," Ruth said.

Oida headed toward them slowly, shading her eyes with one hand, looking toward the ground.

Ruth sang a line, Cora ground out the cigarette, picked up the butt and put it in her pocket. She joined her sister.

"I can't stand it," she said.

"I can't either."

"She was seven years old."

"I know."

"Four wives and her mother's is the one he loses."

"I know. And she took over the kids."

"If he had carved this as deeply as he did the one yesterday, there'd be some sign, some trace left."

"Maybe he learned after losing this one. He didn't want it to happen again."

"Maybe."

They watched their mother coming back, walking slightly sideways down the slope, moving gracefully. They had cleared all the stone now, and together they handswept it clean, blowing the particles away. Cora carried the clumps of grass to the gully, tossed them down into the underbrush.

"One of them's the caretaker, but he doesn't know about the records. He just keeps weeds out."

"You can find out, though," Cora said. "I doubt anyone owns this plot. It's beneath the slope."

"We'll buy it." Ruth brushed her hands, stood up. "We'll just buy it and put up a permanent marker."

Oida was looking at the road. "It was right here. I remember this woman said 'you kiss your momma for the last time, honey,' and I ran. . . ." Oida's voice broke, and she waited a moment. Cora and Ruth looked at one another and then down. "I ran and ran." She pointed behind Ruth. "They were standing there, and I ran from here, around behind, and then I was on the road, right there, and I ran straight down. I remember it was almost straight down."

"Well, Momma, this has got to be it, don't you think?" Cora gestured toward the rock. "I mean, he said it was a big limestone, and this is a big limestone."

"And it's been broken," Ruth added. "Look. And it's right where it would have washed into the gully. I say this is it."

"So do I."

Oida was nodding a little, eyes going from the grave to the road. "But it's been so long."

"This is it, Momma," Cora said.

"We'll get a stone, have one made," Ruth said.

"I think we should keep the limestone too."

"We'll have it put on the other. We'll get a big flat one, put this in the center with her name on it."

Oida stood looking at the stone.

"Please, Momma," one of them said. "Let this be it."

They went directly home from the cemetery. Heat danced on the car, whipped through the window.

Janey and Dellie were sitting in the porch swing. By the front door was a paper bag.

"Pecan pie," Janey said. "Baked it last night."

"So," Dellie said, when they were at the kitchen table again. "You go out to the cemetery today?"

Oida set saucers on the table, began cutting the pie.

"Yes we did," Cora said. "We found Grandma's grave."

"You drove all the way to Greenbriar?"

"Good pie." Ruth pushed a plate toward Cora.

"Oida's always thinking she's found that grave," Janey said.

When Dellie started a gospel, Ruth joined in even before Janey, and then Cora, and finally even Oida, her lips whispering the words. The sun set, the window turned black, while the fan spun the harmony into the evening air.

Cora's Letter

Dear Mother,

From Licklog Holler to the desert country is a long way, much farther than 1500 miles. It is skies away and lands away, and here the blossoms are timid and rush forth only for brief periods and disappear for months, maybe years, and seeds hide themselves in the soil until the rains are deep and constant enough to coax them out.

And it was here, Mother, in this desert country that I met a murderer and I would like to tell you his story, but I can't, because his and mine are as entangled as honeysuckle vines in a quick spring, and the more I read who he is the more I see who I am and I can't disclose that story, can I? Besides, women's stories are not interesting unless they are Mary or Mary Magdalene and I am neither. I don't have the stigmata and I can't ask forgiveness, and I will always go and sin more.

Do you remember when Daddy killed the puppy? It was black and white, wasn't it? with a full drooping happy belly? You said "Argul, we can't keep it. You know I'd be the one to take care of it and I can't handle what I got now." He took it outside, I know. It must have been summer, because the grass was rich and sweet, and I sat down there where he had called me. He said "Your mom says you can't keep it," and then his right hand swung up and lashed down, and he had a hammer in it; then he was swinging the puppy up and back, in a high arc, a slow arc, I remember, and I ran toward the shed and peeked behind it. There was a harrow leaning on the fence, and the puppy was impaled on two of the spikes. That's all I remember, though I must have come back into the house, and you must have cried and railed at him. You cried much, I remember, deep, racking sobs. The women in our family can't cry prettily, I know.

This man, Momma, wasn't anyone I liked. I didn't want to see him, and I even tried not to, but I had to. You see, there had been so many men before him, not all nice, men not nice at all, one too young, far too young, and the last, the one I doted on, well, never mind. So when I saw this older man, with grey hair and unlined skin, and neat clothing, whose flat dark eyes watched me closely, I thought perhaps with a man such as he I could grow older gracefully, be a lady, much like you. Do you remember *My Mother Was a Lady*? I've always loved that song. That and *Little Omie*. "You promised to meet me at Adamson's Springs, bring gold and silver and other fine things." He killed her in the song. They usually do.

That was the summer, too, that Leslie had the abortion. I've seen pictures of aborted babies. I gave her the wedding ring that David gave me. She wanted it. I drove her to the abortion clinic, too. Would you have done that? I suspect so, if you had had to.

I know all your songs by heart, Momma, do you know that? There are about fifty, and I know the words, and how you held each one, and if your voice rose or fell or trembled. You had the most beautiful voice. Of Janey, Dellie, Jimmy, Carl, Allen, Betty–of all your brothers and sisters, you are the one with the voice. I can hear you singing at night in your kitchen, at the stove, or while in the back yard, or dusting the house. I don't recall the smell of food or even of Daddy's whiskey, just you singing all those stories, over and over, the same sad stories, of brothers dead or gone, fathers drunk or dead. Do you know that you left out many of the verses? The ones about money, gardeners, servants. Even in *Babes in the Woods*. Momma, those children were stolen. Why do I remember only that they "wandered away on a bright summer's day, and were lost in the woods, I've heard people say." They were "stolen away," Momma, for money.

People leave out what they don't know or don't want others to know. You left out money, poor woman, working thirty years in a factory with no heat, no cooling, with thread floating through the air to cling to your skin and hair, and still you would talcum your body and wash your face and cook supper and sing. And someone left out Jesus until he was twelve, because that someone didn't want clay pigeons tossed into the air from a roof in Egypt, pigeons that quickened into life and flew away. I liked that story, Momma, much better than the water to wine, or the bear lumbering from the wilderness to eat the children for mocking the prophet. What a cruel god, Momma, you owned as your own.

When my Mary was little, she got afraid of rains. Did I tell you that? That's why I wouldn't let her or Leslie go to church. "Is this a flood?" Mary would say, sitting on the sofa clenching her hands, her fingers pink and white from fear. Then she began not drinking water if she hadn't been holding the glass. "Ghosts," she said, "ghosts will poison the water of sinners." And do you know who the sinners were? Little girls who lied to their parents or who did not "honor their father and mother." She knew all the rules by heart, Momma, by soul. Did you know that when I was little I had to fold all my clothes before bed and put them just so on the chair? That scissors had to be in the back of drawers? That first I said "now I lay me down to sleep, I pray the Lord my soul to keep, if I should die before I wake, I pray the Lord my soul to take," and then I said "Claws, nails, hammer wood, keep me safe, keep me good," because I had two gods even then and I was terrified of them both.

Once Daddy came into my bedroom just for a moment. He lifted back the curtains in the wide doorway and the curtains fell from his broad shoulders like deep green wings.

So I wouldn't let Mary or Leslie go to church, and I told them that no, they wouldn't go to hell, that god would send me instead, and that that was okay by me.

This man I knew, know, this murderer, he left out lots of things. He couldn't say my name. I never told you that, did I? That he called me "pretty lady," or "pretty one," and even when I said "Can't you call me by my name?" he would look at me perplexed, tilting his head, and say "sure," and then never say my name.

Once, when we were standing in my kitchen, wrapped in

towels, I handed him a drink and said "I don't even know who you are, you could be a mass murderer for all I know." He took the drink and said "I'm pretty much the same all the time. What you see is what you get."

That scared me then, Momma, and it scares me now. I think he is pretty much the same all the time.

I know the part about the towel bothers you. That's the kind of thing mothers and daughters don't talk about.

Remember how you said when you married Rufus Argul that you were in love with Argul and ended up living with Rufus? I think Rufus is on the loose again, or was, and is now in jail.

Mary told me all the year that I was writing him in jail that I shouldn't be. She said "he doesn't hear what you say, Momma. He hears what he wants to hear." She's a sweet child, so gentle. We talk about why we should both have known murderers. Mary thinks it's because the women in our family tend to like men and to absolve them of every sin. I suspect she's right.

So many things scare me Momma, and I'm a grown woman. Do you know what Leslie said when she learned the man was a murderer? First she said, "I guess you and Mary are going to die violent deaths." Later she said "Don't be afraid, Momma. If he gets out, I can have him taken care of. I've got some friends." She was so pale that day, so thin, her freckles like a blush across her nose.

How did I do that, Momma? Raise a child who could plan a murder, who could know how to plan a murder?

But then, you must ask yourself how you could raise a child who would sleep with men unmarried, and smoke, and rail against god.

Here, when it rains, it falls in sheets heavy and slashing and sudden, and gone. My back yard this brief time is green, sloping, long and wide like the one back home. I wonder why my yard in this desert looks like yours in the past. I wish you were here, in my kitchen.

This man was writing his own story, Momma. You know how we say "the old Parmenter place," or "up by Cape," or "my cousin Joe"? He never did that. That's why I asked so many questions. "Were you married?" "Where's your wife now?" "Do you have any children?" "How did you make so much money?" "How did you lose it?" and on and on, and he would answer me with no real answer. He had this way of dropping his gaze to the right and swinging it back up when he was saying something to impress me, and I learned what was likely true that way, just as we knew when Daddy whistled *Joley Blonde* he would come home drunk. This man was fond of saying "I could tell you stories," but never a good solid name like Betty, Ruth. He had four daughters, Momma, and many brothers and sisters, and I never heard one solid sound of a being alive until he was in jail and everyone was reading about him in the papers. The women he killed had names. Wouldn't you think that if he were innocent, those names would have been sounded at least once?

Once I said "I'd like to hear you say you didn't do it." "I didn't do it," he said, his voice stretching high like a little boy whining away from a whipping.

I kept thinking he was like a bear, you know, something that would charge me some day from a black direction and I had to be ready, but I know now I can't get ready.

I was making music the night before he was arrested, the night when the television program showed his photograph. Do you think if I weren't the kind of woman who made music, I wouldn't be the kind who met murderers? Some friends and I were playing in a garage, the walls lined with bits of old carpet, and Christmas tree lights twinkling like a fairy room. We were playing blues. The men are all married, don't worry, and they're good men. We just played blues and sang. When I left, I almost went by this man's place, but I didn't. Was that my guardian angel do you think? Remember the picture above my bed in the front bedroom? The little girl on the bridge and the angel whose hand keeps her from falling? The angel was a beautiful young man. They always are, aren't they? I just went home and that's when E.J. called me, to tell me about the program and not to see the man anymore, and to call David right away. E. J. is the one who played guitar and sang gospels when you visited. I guess he's pretty enough to be a guardian angel. I did call David, but he didn't believe me. He said he had seen the show and it wasn't the same man at all. Sounds like David, doesn't it? When I was first dating this man, I asked David to check him out. He said he did, but now I wonder.

Sometimes I pretend that I'm David, having a daughter and an ex-wife both involved with murder, or with murderers. But then David's always been involved, too. I think sometimes how he feels now, how he felt that night he heard the radio call about Richard Safford, who used to stand in our living room and want our Mary; how he heard "Safford. . . murder. . . confess. . . young blonde. . . motel," believing, knowing the girl must be Mary. I can be David then, feeling that weight spread through my chest and my legs, like gravity filling me. I've loved David more since then than I ever did while we were married—more's the pity for us both, I know. You needn't say it.

This man never said he wouldn't hurt me. I told him one day "I think you were going to kill me and still may," and he didn't say no. Once, in a phone call, he said "Remember, I still owe you a dinner." He killed the women who had farewell dinners with him. Mary said he was playing games with me. Leslie said I was a fool to stay in touch with him. David asked me to, though that's a secret.

Do you remember when you caught me in the living room with the Bible and scissors? I was standing by the end table, in the half circle of light on the floor—the floor was linoleum then, wasn't it? and we still had the gas heater in the living room?—and had the Bible tied pendant from a pair of scissors. I had just asked "Will I marry," when you stepped in from the hallway. Your mouth was drawn just a little tight, not full and soft like usual. You said "You'd better be careful asking questions when you don't know who'll be answering." You scared me. That's what you meant to do. That's what this year has been like, holding the Bible by scissors.

There are black holes in space, Momma, and solar winds that

whip through the universe and make it contract. And we're rushing somewhere. There's no god who knows that this man might kill me or that Richard Safford might kill Mary.

Have you noticed that I've aged more quickly than you did? I'm trying hard not to care, but that was another reason for this man. It isn't easy being an older woman in this country. Mary doesn't even wear makeup; Leslie, poor baby, will never know she's pretty until a man who hates her tells her so. That rule's not in the Bible, Momma. I made it up.

I've only dreamed about him once. I was in this gigantic house, it was raining, and he kept pressing his hands and face up to the window. Then I was going down the stairs, and he was coming up, then we were leaning over a long table, but I was on top, and sliding a knife across his throat and he turned into a woman. The police say he's homosexual. I suspect that will bother you some.

Did you watch that special last year, called *Shoah?* The one about the holocaust, the extermination of the Jewish people? I imagine you didn't. You wouldn't have been able to stand it. You would have stood in the kitchen, sipping tea, just listening, thinking you should make yourself watch it, and then you would have suddenly walked up the hallway, into the living room, and snapped off the set. Mary walks like you, and scurries like you when she's upset.

This murderer and I watched that show together. He said that I shouldn't be surprised at the coldness of the people there. He said if I would travel, I would learn that most of the people wanted the Jews gone, no matter the way. He himself was fascinated by the "German machinery," the "precision." "How could they keep all those people from knowing they were going to die?" he asked, and shook his head. The last show, I was at his house, and on the screen was the German system, the trains, the quick shuttling to the decontamination, to the barbers, and he said "See. That's what I mean." The Jewish barbers were talking, about how they did know, they knew why they were cutting those women's hair, but they didn't tell. Remember Simon

Wiesenthal, Momma? He wrote *The Murderers Among Us*. Of all the stories in there, I remember most the one about the little boy who stretched to reach the measuring pole so he could work, not die. Why do I remember that one best?

After he was convicted, on the margin of the letter, scribbled up the side, was "I am innocent of murder." Isn't that an odd postscript after fifty-six letters?

But, Momma, he didn't hurt me. There's the bald truth. One night when I was very lonely and sad, I knocked on his door, and slept by him, and he never touched me. During the night, he lifted the blankets over me and fell back asleep. David used to do that, too. Did Argul? Rufus? Am I scaring you, Momma?

A few weeks after this man was taken to jail, a woman came by to see me. Her name was Naomi and I had met her twice before. She was one of those dark, lithe women, who wear long skirts and soft black sweaters and tie colored bands around their foreheads. She began talking about these men she had stayed with during the summer. She mumbled, just stumbling out a phrase and looking away. She said "Green River murderer," and a few minutes later "necromancy." I know this is a college town, Momma, and a new age, but that's part of what she said. The rest was a jumble about a van, and being afraid, and women's bodies with no visible sign of death. The next time she came, I was so trembly that I sent her away. If I turned away an angel in disguise, I'm not sorry.

This last week, a San Diego detective came by my house. He says he's hiring a psychic to find the victims. I told him about Naomi, and he was startled. He said the police have never released the information about the deaths. He didn't ask me for Naomi's full name, Momma, or her address. They never want all the stories.

When I was little, I thought my rhymes would keep me alive until morning when I could see the enemy. Now I'm not so sure. That's one reason I wanted to tell this man's story, because that's rather like a long rhyme, with reason, that would enchant him away. But when I began reading his letters, I knew I couldn't tell the story, not all of it, and only in a letter to you. You see, he wants his story told. All that time, I thought I was visiting him and writing him for David and all the Marys. I thought the police would take all the letters, all the notes, and make a book and that men of learning would study it and see the truth. They didn't, though, not even David. The district attorney told me what would be acceptable and what wouldn't. I think I answered four questions.

When I went to the trial, one of the mothers was there. She's small, with dark cropped hair and she cried all the time. She said "You may not know it, but I saved your life." I said "I know it." "Walk in faith," she told me. And I said "That's hard to do." It is, Momma, hard to do.

Yesterday, one of this man's friends asked me if I was writing a book, and said that he wanted to relay my answer. I said no. I can't ever tell anyone because in one of the first letters from jail, he said "I hope you're saving everything. We'll need them later." In those letters, Momma, are all these stories, of this compassionate son, of this seer, this psychic, this economist, this philosopher, this companion of the idle rich, the Mafia, the protector of the justly accused. He was recreating himself for the world. In the beginning, I suppose, is always the word, but I'll not be the one who starts it.

He was very proud that he was not a sex offender. When he was convicted, and they moved him upstairs, he called and said he was "where he belonged, with men, real men." "They may be murderers," he said, "but they're men."

I want someone to know he said that.

I saw two psychiatrists before I wrote the last letter and asked him not to contact me again. One psychiatrist said he could not help me at all, but he was very interested in the story. The other was the man who talked to David about Richard Safford. He asked me more questions than the police ever did. He said that if I wanted to be safe, I had to give the power to the murderer, that when I wrote the letter, I had to remind him of his promise to me that he wanted what was best for me, I had to relinquish the power to him, to say that I knew he could find me if he wanted, but that I hoped he didn't, that I trusted him to keep his word. Does that sound familiar to you, Momma? It did to me. And what scares me most is that I did as I was instructed. Somewhere, in some prison I cannot see, is a man who holds my petition in his hand and I want it back.

I guess I'll go now, Momma. It's a grey day, a thin day, the sky sort of stingy. I'm tired and a little restless. Just recently another little girl here was raped and killed. The man's last name is Bible, and that's troubling me. Maybe playing and singing for a while will ease my mind. Mary's learning all your songs. Her voice is much like yours, high and sweet, and I'm so glad, since you can't sing any more. Leslie's is lower, more like mine, but she has a sad tone. They're good girls, both of them.

You take care. I love you.

Cora

A Note about the Author

R. M Kinder was born in Bloomfield, in the bootheel of Missouri, where these stories are set. She received her B.A. and M.F.A. in creative writing from the University of Arizona in Tucson. While there she studied under Robert C. S. Downs, C. E. Poverman, Jonathan Penner, and Vance Bourjaily, and won the Fred Scott Award for Fiction. She completed her Ph.D. in rhetoric and composition in the summer of 1990 at the University of Arizona and is a member of Phi Beta Kappa. Currently she is an assistant professor of English at Central Missouri University, teaching creative writing and teacher education courses. She recently became co-editor of *Pleiades* (Central's literary journal) and associate editor of *Publications of the Missouri Philological Association*. Her stories have appeared in *New Times*, *Cottonwood Review*, *Puerto del Sol*, *Primavera*, *Cimarron Review*, *The Nebraska Review*, *Dickinson Review* Belle Lettres Society, and others. *Sweet Angel Band* is her first book.